Blue Ridge
BLESSINGS

Blue Ridge BLESSINGS

An Inspirational Romance

Joan B. Clark

Chapter One

everend Lucas Lee Carson II, the newly arrived pastor of the Community Church in Loch James, Virginia, stepped off the porch of the Victorian manse whistling, headed for his church down the block. The 36-year-old preacher was not wearing a clerical outfit today. Dressed in old khaki clothes and work shoes, he planned to plant a dozen rosebushes outside his study window. These bushes had arrived just yesterday from Jackson &Perkins Nursery in Oregon, a dozen assorted hybrids—a gift from his mother to celebrate his new pastorate.

Few people were up and about this early and he enjoyed the quiet summer view of the Blue Ridge Mountains. When he had driven along the Blue Ridge Parkway for his interview weekend in the spring, the flowering dogwood, azaleas, and rhododendron bushes the size of trees stretched as far as the eye could see. The sheer beauty of the place reassured him that his search to find a rural environment in which to raise his children was a worthy effort. When young, he had enjoyed hiking with his botanist father who taught him to recognize flowers and herbs. Somehow Baltimore, where he'd just finished being an assistant in a large interdenominational church, did not provide the mountains and the streams he preferred for himself and his children. This rural setting in Loch James seemed safer and healthier.

Luke had rolled up his sleeves for working, and with his six-foot height and broad shoulders, he looked like an athlete. When a mockingbird answered his whistle, Luke laughed out loud. Grateful that Aunt Lydia was coping well with the last of the unpacking, he was free to pursue his gardening hobby in this two-week getting-settled period before he retrieved the twins from his mother's home in Baltimore.

Luke (or Pastor Luke as he liked his congregation to call him) had already dug the twelve holes and was unwrapping the protective materials from around the first rosebush, a red "Mister Lincoln" when he heard the clip-clop of a horse's hooves coming up the maple tree-lined approach road to the church. The unusual sound drew his attention to a bright yellow, two-wheeled pony cart containing a petite, dark-haired woman in faded jeans, a bright red tee-shirt, and a ponytail. She handled the reins masterfully as she pulled around the corner of the church, unloaded some artist's supplies, unhooked the pony, and then literally put him out to pasture on the back lawn.

Oh, yes, he thought, *this must be the French artist they told me was going to paint a mural of Christ with the children on the back wall of the church. She looks like a teenager-- busy and energetic.* He watched her sling a pouch over her shoulder and climb up the scaffolding erected yesterday by the men of the Building and Grounds Committee.

She must be fifteen feet off the ground, he marveled. He shaded his eyes to look up and watch her sketch in charcoal on the white stucco surface. As she leaned out to stretch a line, the scaffolding began to sway and the scraping sound again claimed his attention. She agilely shifted her weight, but by then Luke was already on his feet and racing toward the scaffolding.

"Hold on!" he shouted. The loud command startled the woman so that she lost her footing and, despite a desperate clutching for a handhold, she began to fall. Instinctively, Luke reached out to catch her in his arms and they both landed on the ground.

"Are you all right?" he asked when he'd gotten his breath back. "Why, you don't weigh much more than one of my twins!" Luke observed.

"Mon Dieu! Why did you shout at me so? You caused me to lose my balance!" she scolded with a pointed finger.

"I heard the scaffolding rubbing and saw it begin to sway," he replied defensively.

"That is nothing. Scaffolding tends to sway, but you frightened me and I slipped and fell." Her dark eyes fairly snapped with indignation. She straightened her tee-shirt and brushed off her jeans.

"I'm sorry," he apologized and helped her to her feet. She had to tilt her head to look up to him. Her dark eyes bore into his blue ones.

"Well, go back to your landscaping and leave me to work in peace," and she gave him a definite push. Luke, feeling foolish, took his time returning to his rose bushes. Somehow he couldn't help glancing over regularly to where the artist was working. She might be dressed like a teenager, but having held her in his arms, he knew she was very much a woman.

Shame on you! He chided himself. Then he immediately forgave himself for noticing an attractive woman. *After all, thirty-six is not old and Emily has been dead for eleven years. I wonder what her name is. I'm sure I'd have remembered if I met her on my interview visit.*

An hour later, Luke was watering his new bed of roses with a hose when he felt a gentle tap on his arm. He whirled around to find the petite artist looking up at him. Luke shut off the hose and waited.

Apologetically, she said, "I forgot to thank you for catching me and saving me from getting hurt. Would you like to share lunch? As usual, Mammy Lizzie has packed enough food for two people. She worries that I don't eat enough."

Intrigued, he thanked her. "I didn't know people still have mammies.' Thought that had gone out with the Civil War. May I contribute some cold lemonade from my thermos bottle?"

"That sounds good," she accepted while she spread a blanket in a sheltered corner of the churchyard and began to unpack a large picnic basket. Luke sat down, and she handed him a fried chicken leg. He hesitated a moment and then asked, "What is your name? Are you famous?"

"I hope to be famous so the whole world will someday know the name of Aimee St. Claire. My 'Smiling Christ with the Children' mural may be a big step toward that. Now, I know you're a landscaper, but what's your name?" she asked in return.

Luke paused a moment. It was refreshing to be considered just a man, not a clergyman, for once. Although it went against his usual formal nature, he decided impulsively to omit his title for the time being. "Luke Carson," he answered and waited to see if she would recognize the name and automatically distance herself from him. When she just reached over and warmly shook hands, Luke said grace for his food silently.

Over the cheese and home baked bread, Aimee bragged that her Clem and Lizzie kept goats and made this incredibly delicious goat cheese. Luke agreed that its taste was marvelous and wondered out loud if he should call her Heidi like the youthful heroine of the Swiss mountains. She laughed and let him know that Clem's claim to local fame is in his taking goat milk to the hospitals for premature infants.

"How long have you lived here?" he asked here.

"I was born here and aside from three years with my father's French relatives in Paris, I've always lived here. Father was a French landscape painter who met my mother at an artists' colony one summer near here. They fell in love and he built her the mountain house I live in now. He even gave art classes in this very church. Of course, he died five years ago while I was abroad. Then Mother became an invalid, and I came home to help Lizzie care for her until she died last year. That's my whole history. I do religious art to pay my bills, but eventually, I want to paint landscapes and portraits of the mountain folk. I give some sketching classes on my veranda in good weather."

After they had lingered over grapes and homemade gingersnap cookies, Aimee repacked the few leftovers in the basket. Then he helped her shake out and refold the blanket.

"I'm sorry to run," she explained, "but I need to take advantage of the sun before it moves around to the other side of the church building and there are too many shadows where I'm working. Thanks again."

Luke found himself wishing she wouldn't go. "How about my supplying lunch tomorrow—same time, same place?" he offered.

Not missing a beat, Aimee added, "Good, and bring some more of that delicious lemonade, will you?" He nodded and then shook his head as he watched her climb back up the scaffolding in her sure-footed tennis shoes. She climbed like a monkey, so graceful and lithe.

By two o'clock Aimee was gone, and Luke had decided to add a border to his new rose garden tomorrow—*to make a more finished effect,* he told himself as he headed home to pick up the car for the trip to the local nursery for plants.

As he came into the kitchen, Lydia asked, "Didn't you get hungry around noon today, Luke? I was expecting you for lunch."

"I'm sorry. I should have called you, but I did have lunch….with a most beautiful young lady."

"You're joking, Luke! I wish you would start dating. The twins need a mother."

"I have to tell you, Lydia, Aimee doesn't exactly look motherly."

"Aimee who?" interrogated Lydia, intrigued by his obvious and unusual interest in a woman.

"You asked me about lunch. She shared her lunch with me."

"Oh ho, so how did that come about? Is she a parishioner?"

"No, she's the artist I caught in my arms when she fell off the scaffolding."

"Stop your joshing, Luke."

"You know me, Lydia. I'm perfectly serious. She's the artist who's painting the church mural."

"Oh yes, I read about her in last week's LOCH JAMES SENTINAL. She's French, but they didn't say she was beautiful."

"She is and I'll need a nice lunch for two tomorrow—tuna fish sandwiches and a bowl of your potato salad? Maybe some sliced tomatoes and how about sponge cake for dessert?"

"My gracious, if I can promote this romance with my cooking, so be it," Lydia enthused. "I'm not totally used to this kitchen yet, but I can whip up a gourmet lunch to impress this new lady in your life."

"Let's not go overboard, Lydia. We spent an hour together and she doesn't even know I'm a clergyman yet." Luke started to head out to the garage to forestall any more questions.

"Oh, Luke, I just discovered the name of an old college friend on your Board of Elders. There can't be two men named 'Jackson Montgomery.' We used to call him 'Monty' at the College of William and Mary. He was editor of the yearbook and I was a staff photographer. Imagine finding a friend after thirty years in this little place! I wonder if we'll even recognize each other when we meet. Maybe I'd better set an appointment to have my hair done. I don't suppose you know if he's married?"

"There is a 'Monty' on my Board who owns some coal mines, I think. He was away in Europe when I interviewed, but no one has mentioned his wife, Lydia. You're quite a romantic." He laughed and again headed for the garage.

Lydia looked after him and thought, *Thank you, God. Luke actually looks happy today.*

Luke was unloading the anemone and potentilla plants from the back of his trusty blue Volvo station wagon by eight-thirty the next morning. He began marking with pegs and strings to be sure the border would be precisely straight. Next, he unloaded the white wrought iron bench and placed it under the closest live oak tree with a clear view of both his rose garden and her mural.

By nine-thirty, Luke was becoming impatient because Aimee was late. Yesterday she'd been at work by nine. *Where in tarnation is she?"* he fretted to himself. *Why does it matter to me so much?* He wondered.

Just past ten o'clock he heard the faint hoof beats and found himself heaving a sigh of relief. When Aimee stopped the pony cart, Luke was there to unhitch the pony and help carry her cans of paint, pallets, and brushes. "Good morning," she greeted him cheerfully. "It's beautiful painting weather," she continued.

"You're late!" he chided her.

"Who says I'm late?" she retorted. "I don't have any set hours. I'm not punching any time clock."

"Well. I was excepting you sooner," he said truculently. "I was afraid you'd hurt your back or legs in that fall yesterday when you didn't come by nine."

"No. It just takes time to mix the paint. Then the sheep got out. One of those dang geese opened the latch on the gate and then had fun chasing them. It took the dog, Clem, and me an hour to get them corralled again. I begin adding colors today," she explained as she unrolled a colored illustration of the entire mural.

"Is this what the finished mural will look like?" Luke asked while studying the small painting.

"More or less. If I get inspired, I may make some adjustments, but basically, this is what has been approved," she answered.

"Maybe God will provide inspiration for Christ's face," Luke suggested.

She looked at him strangely. "Maybe so, but the Man Upstairs and I haven't done much talking for a long time. Thanks for helping me unload. I'll see you at lunchtime. You did bring us lunch, didn't you?"

"Of course I did… as I said I would. The coolers are over there in the shade by the new bench."

"Oh yes, I noticed that bench coming in. 'Nice landscaping touch," she complimented him. Well, let's get to work," and she began to climb the scaffolding.

I'm NOT going to watch her climb this time, Luke told himself sternly and returned to his planting. *If Aimee needs help, I'm within hailing distance.*

At noon sharp, they met at the new bench under the huge live oak. Luke unpacked Lydia's promised gourmet lunch—salmon salad, crusty Italian bread, sliced tomatoes and cucumber in sour cream flavored with dill, and for dessert…green grapes and sponge cake. Their cool drink was raspberry iced tea.

They talked during lunch. "Tell me about your geese," he said. "I didn't know geese could open gates."

"Well, geese are very clever and in Europe, they're used to guard cattle and children.

The German Army even used mean geese on patrol. Mine aren't mean, just mischievous, so we've put a lock on the corral gate now. Clem will be laughing about it tonight, but he sure wasn't happy this morning. 'Says he's too old to be bamboozled by a couple of geese."

"When my children come," Luke said, "I know they'll be fascinated by your geese."

"You said they were eleven years old?"

"Yes…twins, a boy and a girl. We call them Andy and Mandy."

"Those are their real names?"

"No, they were christened Andrew and Amanda."

"What does their mother call them?"

Luke's face fell. "Emily died giving birth to them."

"I'm sorry," Aimee said, regretting having reminded him of his grief. She reached over and patted his hand in sympathy.

"Don't be. You couldn't have known. My mother's sister, Lydia, who was a new widow when they were born, came to help me and has stayed on with us. She's the one who packed our lovely lunch."

"Thank her for me. Everything was absolutely delicious!"

Luke changed the subject. "Tell me how painting on an outside wall differs from painting on canvas," he inquired.

"It'll use gallons of oil paint because the wall is so porous. To make sure it looks good from a distance, I'll mix in a lot of yellows with almost all tints and not use white at all or very sparingly. The paint will be so thick that I'll use a palette knife to spread it for the shadows."

"So you learned to do murals in France?"

"Yes. One of my instructors did one on a country church in southern France near the Italian border and I assisted him. It's hard work, and I often have an audience. People like to stand around and watch."

"My kids sure will, especially Andy."

"Why Andy?" she asked.

"He is the artistic one and Mandy is the athletic one. She comes close to beating me at tennis already. I'll be going to Baltimore this weekend to retrieve them from a visit with their grandparents, my mother, and my father. Although they keep things lively, I really miss them. My father promised to take them to Washington, D.C. to see the Capitol and Smithsonian Institute."

"They must be bright kids if they're interested in the Smithsonian. It's good they get to know their grandparents," she approved.

"I promised to take them through the Battlefield Park at Appomattox Courthouse on our way home here. How about local tennis courts?" he asked.

"There are some at the high school, but they're not used much except when school is in session. A couple of the bigger houses have their own, but they're not public."

"How about shopping?" Luke asked. "Where do folks go when they want something besides gas and groceries?"

"Probably Lebanon or Abingdon. They both have malls. Then there's always mail order and email shopping. The same UPS trucks that deliver the nursery plants all over bring other stuff in from larger places. I order my art supplies from New York City, for instance. We may be rural, but we're not backward."

"Have you ever thought about marrying again, Luke?" Aimee asked.

"It took me nearly five years to get used to Emily's being gone. We had so much in common and we were high school sweethearts. Now I have two wonderful children who take up most of my spare time. Frankly, I haven't met a woman who appeals to me. How about you? You're an attractive woman. How come you're still single?"

"You haven't much time to date when you're nursing your sick mother for four years. My French boyfriend found someone else. Now I'm trying to make up for lost time establishing my art career. Nor have I met a man in whom I'm especially interested." *Until now*, she added to herself. "Besides, the local guys are mostly taken. My timing is off, I guess," she said wistfully.

"In God's own time, there'll be someone for you, Aimee," Luke comforted her.

"And also for you, Luke, I hope," she responded as they cleared away the lunch and returned to their respective tasks.

Chapter Two

The sky was overcast on Thursday when Aimee and Luke arrived to begin their various tasks at nine o'clock. "Good morning", she greeted him.

"That's not what the weatherman forecast on the news this morning", he replied.

"Oh, what are they calling for?"

"Scattered showers. Don't you listen to the radio in the morning?" he asked.

"No. I like to listen to the birds. Clem didn't say anything about his rheumatism bothering him either," Aimee explained. "Showers will be good for your new plants, but I can't paint in the rain. If it does rain, I'll have the rest of the day off."

Luke industriously went on trimming the overgrown hedge and long-neglected lilac. Aimee checked the sky from the scaffolding a half hour later and decided the dark clouds did indeed look ominous, so she began putting lids back on paint cans and storing them in the shed.

Suddenly, large raindrops began plopping about them. "C'mon, Aimee, run for it…into the vestibule." He grabbed her hand and they ran together.

She was laughing and breathless as they burst into the outer entrance room of the church. "Let's wait here until this downpour lets up," Luke suggested.

"Whew, that's one fast way to cool off!" Aimee commented. Her dark hair was curly from the extra moisture and a few drops glinted on her eyelashes. His shirt was wet and clung to his strong arms and broad chest she noticed as he smiled down at her.

I'd like to capture Luke's smile on Christ's face in the mural, especially that warm and kind expression. Jesus was a young carpenter, so he undoubtedly had strong arms, too, Aimee thought to herself.

"You said if it rained, you'd have the rest of the day off," Luke reminded Aimee.

"So what are your plans for the rest of the day? Are you going home to work on portraits or landscapes?"

"Maybe. I really hadn't thought that far ahead." Then she impulsively added "Would you like to see where I live in the mountains? I'm sure Lizzie would fix us both a nice hot bowl of soup for lunch."

"I really would like to see your home, those geese, and meet that mammy of yours," Luke responded.

"Clem and she are my family now," Aimee said seriously. "I don't know what I'd do without them."

"I couldn't stay very long since I have many things to attend to this afternoon," Luke cautioned her, "but hot soup sounds good after this soaking. Do I have time to run home and change into dry things? You really need to, too."

"I'll draw you a map and then you can come in time for lunch. I'll have time to get into dry things and warn Lizzie we're having company for lunch." Aimee borrowed a visitor's card and pencil from the rack by the entrance, turned it over, and rapidly sketched a map starting from the only signal light in the center of town.

"Go west underneath the Blue Ridge Parkway and keep on about two and a half miles. On the right, you'll spot our mailbox next to the pasture for retired racehorses. There's even a horse painted on the mailbox. Turn into our lane and you'll see our log house up on the knoll. The geese will let us know you've come. 'Better stay in the car until I can come out and rescue you."

"It sounds exciting," and Luke grinned. "Well, the rain has stopped, so you can be on your way. I'll be along in about an hour."

As Luke hurried home, he thought about what he could say to Lydia who would be sure to tease him about eating lunch again with Aimee. He decided that his best defense was a good offense. "You'll never guess where I'm going for lunch," he teased Lydia.

"You're eating with the mayor and his wife?" Lydia guessed.

"No."

"How about the police chief?" she guessed again. Luke shook his head and grinned.

Finally, Lydia said, "Not with that cute French artist again?"

"You found me out. She even has a mammy who I'm going to meet."

"You're going to her home for lunch? 'Fast work, Luke. Where does she live anyway?"

"Somewhere up in the mountains. She drew me a map."

"Well, don't you get lost," Lydia warned. "I'll be waiting to hear all about it at supper. You'd better get dried off and cleaned up. Actually, with you gone for lunch, I'll be able to get the children's rooms ready sooner. All their books, clothes, and toys are still in boxes. I want to get Mandy's tennis awards up and Andy's framed art works so the twins will feel at home right away when they arrive this weekend. When you get home, you can help me with the rugs."

"How about doing that now?" he asked.

"Oh no, you run along and get cleaned up for your lunch date."

"All right, but it's not a date, Lydia," he protested. "We're just friends."

In half an hour Luke was on his way dressed in his least faded jeans, a clean tee shirt, waterproof

Jacket, and his old comfortable riding boots. The car windows were down and he was whistling to accompany a tape of Gospel hymns. After he passed under the highway, he began to watch his mileage gauge as he motored through woods on both sides of the macadam road.

Suddenly he emerged from the woods to a beautiful cleared pasture on his right with six thoroughbreds. Several were drinking from a small pond, and two had come to the fence when they'd heard his motor. Among the horses were about a dozen sheep adding to the pastoral scene.

He turned right at the expected horse-embellished mailbox and bounced along a lane which climbed gradually. Looking forward, he spotted a large log cabin home with a wide veranda running its full length. This was no pioneer house, but modern, gabled home. Why, the porch was at least ten feet wide. Somehow he'd pictured Aimee in a smaller, more primitive setting.

As he turned off the engine and smoothed his hair, he waited for her to appear. The geese were already scolding and looking mean. As soon as Aimee stepped out onto the porch, he called, "Help! Save me from these killer geese." She started to laugh and Clem came around the corner of the house waving his hat and shooing the big birds.

"It's OK now, sir," Clem said. Aimee reached the blue Volvo at about the same time.

"Come on out, Luke, and meet Clem," she said. "Clem, this is Luke. He's fixing up the church grounds and we both got rained out today, so I invited him for lunch."

"Pleased to meet you, Clem," Luke said and extended his hand. Hesitantly, the tall black man with kinky white hair shook Luke's hand. "Thanks for saving me from the geese, Clem," Luke said.

"When you get used to them, geese aren't so fierce," Clem replied. He stepped back deferentially to let Aimee and her guest precede him up the three wooden steps to the long porch.

"Gracious," said Luke," you can see forever from here!"

"The veranda wraps to the other side, too," Aimee said, so we can watch both sunrise and sunsets. They strolled together to the corner and suddenly Luke stopped.

"Aimee, look at this spectacular rainbow!"

"Yes, Luke, let's watch it for a few minutes because it won't last long," she replied.

"It reminds me also," Luke quoted from Revelation 4:3, "There was a rainbow around the throne in appearance like an emerald."

"My father," Aimee said, "was a painter, you know, and he considered a rainbow the most beautiful combination of colors anywhere. His watercolor scenes often featured rainbows over these mountains."

Luke said, "I think of Noah and the story of the ark when God promised with a rainbow never to flood the whole earth again."

"That's right," she agreed. "Lizzie used to read me children's Bible stories. She told me that anytime I see a rainbow, it's to remind me that God is good."

Luke silently added to himself, *Thank-you, God, that Aimee is acquainted with the Bible.*

"Will your mural contain a rainbow?" he asked aloud.

"There isn't one in the preliminary sketch, but now that you mention it, I think a rainbow would be appropriate in the mural." She looked toward him. "You're smiling, Luke. I enjoy watching nature in any form from here, too—even thunderstorms with their lightning bolts are spectacular."

They watched together as the colors of the rainbow faded, and they heard a bell sound.

"What's that?" asked Luke.

"That means lunch is ready. Clem's getting hard of hearing, so Lizzie calls us to meals with an old school marm's bell," Aimee explained. "C'mon inside and meet Lizzie."

"Something smells wonderful!" Luke commented as he stepped into the hallway. The ceiling was eight feet tall, and a set of steps on his left probably led to bedrooms upstairs. On the walls were shelves for kerosene lamps, but the hallway was actually lit by a modern chandelier.

"The kitchen is back this way," Aimee directed. They emerged into a large, square room featuring an eight-foot pine table, highly polished, with six caned chairs around it.

Woven placemats, undoubtedly done in natural dyes by local craftspeople, complimented the shiny surface. A huge soup tureen with matching ladle was already steaming by one of the places.

"Mammy, this is Luke, the one I told you about. He saved me from a nasty fall!"

"Luke, meet Lizzie."

"Glad to meet you, Luke," said the short, stocky black woman wearing a black dress that complimented her grizzled hair. When she smiled, her whole face lit up.

"Thanks for saving our missy! We've wanted to meet you, and I'd have cooked a whole dinner if I'd had more time."

Noticing that only two places were set at the table, Aimee ordered, "Lizzie, put on two more places. I want Clem and you to eat with us."

Clem chimed in, "No, Miss Aimee, I think that'd not be proper."

Luke immediately stepped in, "Please, I want to get to know both of you. Maybe when my children come, you'll get to meet them, too. Please."

Aimee said, "Let me set the two places and you bring the corn bread, Mammy. That's how it's going to be."

With no further argument, the four stood for a short grace by Lizzie, then sat down to heavy pottery bowls full of pea and ham soup. There were butter and honey for the cornbread. The heavy glass water goblets were antique as were the pewter eating utensils and water pitcher. As they ate, Luke registered that the log walls were plastered between logs, and casement windows opened onto a screened part of the back porch. A modern electric stove, refrigerator, and dishwater together with a stainless steel sink occupied one side of the room. On the other was a stone fireplace with antique andirons. A sitting area containing a television set and telephone was defined by a large oval braided rug that Lizzie had made herself. This gave a warm look to the waxed hardwood floor, Burlap drapes could be pulled across to keep out the cold. Obviously, this country kitchen was the hub of the house.

Luke helped himself to a second serving of cornbread and asked Lizzie, "How do you make this cornbread? It is absolutely delicious."

Aimee spoke up to answer, "Mammy keeps her recipe a secret, but I know that when she makes it, she adds some cooked rice and corn kernels."

For dessert, Lizzie served baked custard sprinkled with nutmeg and passed caramel sauce. Large sugar cookies made their rounds to go with mugs of hot tea. Luke felt at home with these hospitable folks and was now even surer that his children would love Aimee and her household.

"Would you like to see the rest of the place, Luke?" Aimee asked as they rose from the table.

Clem added, "Don't forget the barns and animals, Aimee."

"I saw some horses and sheep in the pasture as I turned into your lane," Luke responded. "Do you always keep them together?"

"You don't where you come from?" Aimee asked. "I notice you're wearing riding boots."

"There aren't many sheep in tidewater Virginia," he replied.

"Well, we do that so when the old horses get skittish during summertime storms or at night, the sheep calm them. We don't ride those horses except to exercise them at a gentle gait. They've earned their retirement."

As they came down the porch stairs, Luke looked cautiously around for the attack geese. Aimee grinned. "Don't worry about Greta and Gilbert. They're hanging around the back door waiting for table scraps from lunch," she assured him. "Besides, now they know you're a friend. These geese are very intelligent." They went on to the barns.

"All the stalls are empty, but we'll walk through and out the other side to see Clem's goats. She pointed out the tack room full of equipment and the big refrigerators and dishwashers in the cheese-making area as they passed them.

Six frisky spotted goats cavorted in a large fenced pasture just outside. One posed on top of a large rock as if daring any of the others to push her off. Then she leaped from there to the roof of a low shed when she saw humans approaching.

"How does Clem get these goats to stand still for milking?" asked Luke.

"He has to lure them into the barn and tie them to yoke. Then wearing sterile gloves, he washes their udders with an antiseptic solution and milks them into stainless steel buckets. Clem got into this when the hospital people needed something besides cow's milk for premature infants.

The Health Department inspects us regularly for cleanliness and the vet verifies the health of the goats."

Clem joined them and added, "When the vet comes, I always give him two packages of feta cheese for his wife."

Aimee explained, "The cheese is a cash crop for Clem. He also sells his carvings to tourists."

"Oh?" said Luke. "What do you carve—goats?"

"Sometimes…and geese, bears, and the thoroughbreds, "Clem answered. "The Loch James and Roanoke gift shops sell them on consignment to tourists."

"Would you like to see the chicken and the rabbits? Aimee asked.

Luke glanced at his watch. "Thanks, but I think I'd better get going. There are things to be done before I go back to Baltimore this weekend to bring the twins home here. Thanks for a lovely lunch and I'm really impressed with your 'Painter's Pond'. By the way, where is the pond?"

"It is formed from a spring that feeds my waterfall back up the hill and then becomes the brook running through the pastures. Didn't you hear the waterfall when we're on the porch?"

"No, I didn't. 'Guess I was too taken with the rainbow. Maybe you'll let me come again and bring the children?" Luke asked. "This is a beautiful place—so peaceful. You must hate to leave it, Aimee."

She shrugged. "Well, one has to make a living, Luke. At least, I make my living doing something I really like."

Just then Lizzie called from the porch, "There's a fellow from Roanoke on the phone for you, Aimee."

"I'm coming, Lizzie. This may be a go-ahead call for another mural in Roanoke," she said excitedly. "I'll see you tomorrow, Luke." She hurried into the house and Luke took a last long look at this peaceful mountain home. Then he waved goodbye to Clem as he drove out of the yard.

Aimee picked up the phone. "Yes?"

"This is Rev. Jedediah Smith at the First Baptist Church in Roanoke. Our Board met last night and has OK'd the mural for the fellowship hall, the one that illustrates the Parable of the Prodigal Son. They've agreed to the deposit of $300, so please send us a contract. By the way, Father Richter of Holy Nativity Episcopal Church says they may want a mural, too, but he's going to wait and see what ours looks like first. They're pretty conservative, you know, "and he laughed. "How soon can you start?"

"It will have to be late August. Is that all right?" Aimee asked. He agreed.

"Thank you for calling. I will send you the contract this week." Aimee hung up and then grabbed Lizzie to do a wild dance around the kitchen.

"Papa would be so proud of me! I inherited his talent and even studied where he did."

Lizzie said, "Thank the Lord for all His blessings, child."

Aimee added, "I can't wait to tell Luke tomorrow!"

"That Luke is a mighty handsome man," Lizzie said.

Aimee flushed and parried with, "Oh, Lizzie. There's more to life than getting married. Quit trying to pair me off. The last time it was the vet's intern and he kept wanting me to go to horse shows with him. This guy is a glorified gardener. He's a friend and a nice person, but that's the extent of it."

"If you say so…" Lizzie said and sat down in her rocker to rest before starting supper preparations.

—⁓—

As Luke and Lydia sat having coffee and pound cake for dessert after supper together, Lydia said, "Do you realize you've talked my ear off, Luke, about Aimee and her 'Painter's Pond'? I take it you're very impressed with her housekeeper's lunch, the sentinel geese, Clem's cheese-making and carving, etc. but what about the lady herself?"

Luke blushed like a teenager. "Oh, Lydia, this was almost like my first date. The Lord sent His rainbow like a personal sign to me that I will be happy and He'll bless my ministry here."

"Amen!" added Lydia. "I have already noticed how fresh and clean the air is and how quiet Loch James is. The mailman came right up to the door to leave our mail. I think I'm going to enjoy small-town living. I'm even considering putting in a kitchen garden for fresh herbs and our own tomatoes. There's a place in the back yard that used to be a small garden. 'Nothing like fresh-picked parsley and you can keep raising radishes and lettuce all summer long."

"I'm not sure the twins value vegetables much, Lydia, but you're welcome to try. There's an electric cultivator someone left in the shed, so I'll turn over the soil for you tomorrow. Right now I need to put the finishing touches on my sermon for Sunday. Although it's a summer service, I expect quite a few parishioners who will be there out of curiosity about their new pastor. I'll need to start learning all their names," and he sighed. "I hope they'll be willing to wear name tags for a while until I figure out who is married to whom and which children belong to them."

Lydia said, "Maybe you'll get some invitations to free dinners, but don't take Andy and Mandy. It'll be too hard for them."

"You're probably right on that, Lydia. My children mix well, but people expect a lot from preachers' kids."

On Thursday morning, Aimee was roughly sketching in Jesus and the children with a rainbow over their heads.

"I see you did decide to add a rainbow," Luke said.

"If the church authorities don't like the rainbow, I can easily convert the background to clouds," she replied. "Are the figures in the right proportions—not too big for this wall?"

Luke stepped back and considered the drawing. "No, they look fine to me. Say, what time did you start sketching this morning?"

"Seven o'clock. I couldn't sleep and decided to get going right away. The weather today promises to be really good for painting. When I stop for lunch, I hope to have the face of Christ done. How about his having brown hair and beard? Lizzie likes you, so she's made a splendid lunch for us."

"Brown sounds right. 'See you later.'"

At lunchtime, Luke rinsed his hands off with the hose and joined Aimee on the new bench. As they munched egg salad sandwiches on wheat bread with crisp homemade pickles, Aimee told Luke about some of the more prominent townspeople.

"Dr. Mark Stewart and his wife, Millie, are really nice people. He was the one who got the preemie unit going at the hospital, and she was a social worker before they got married. She still helps a lot of people."

"Do they have children?" Luke asked.

"Sure. Dylan is a carbon copy of his father… a nice young fellow. He attends the University of Virginia in Charlotte and comes home most weekends. Then they have a much younger daughter, Debbie—probably about the same age as your twins."

"The pharmacist owns the drugstore. Mort Culpepper must be seventy-five if he's a day—lends folks money if they can't afford their prescriptions. 'I won't need money in heaven,' he tells people. When he was recovering from surgery last winter, everybody sent in soup and casseroles. When he got better, he threw a party for the whole town. Almost all the teenagers have worked for him as their first job, so he had a trained volunteer staff to keep the drugstore open while he was sick."

"Then there's Belle Miller who runs Belle's Café and Gift Shop which used to be her father's diner. Old Chester used to let all the elderly retirees congregate for free coffees and he never turned a hobo or hitchhiker away. Then Belle comes back from Ashville, North Carolina, and she prettiest up the place and turns all the 'riff-raff', as she calls them, out. Then she adds a lot of tourist souvenirs and calls it Belle's Café and Gift Shop. Needless to say, she's not too popular with the older men, but she does serve good food. She kept the cook, but he's had to learn to make a lot of little fancy salads and sandwiches. If she'd changed his hamburgers or sweet potato and chocolate pecan pies, she might have been run out of town."

Luke laughed and allowed, "Only in a small town!"

"Then there's our banker, Lionel Crapsey," Aimee continued in describing denizens of the town.

I probably should interrupt her, Luke told himself when he heard his Senior Elder's name, *but I'm curious as to what Aimee thinks about him.*

"He's a banker who regularly wears a suit and a hat and drives an expensive car. 'Better not get behind on your mortgage or he'll foreclose. I have no quarrel with him, especially since he's paying for this memorial mural in memory of his wife. He and his daughter Caroline, live in a large Victorian house called Belle's Café out on the lake shore. His wife collected antiques and every year, used to show them off at a Christmas Open House. It's the grandest house in Loch James. They only had one daughter, so Caroline was sent to Sweet Briar College and has never worked a day in her life. She considers herself the belle of Loch James because she is pretty and dresses to kill. However, I pity the man she marries. She was fairly nice when we went to school together, but now that we're grown, she's something else. 'Course you'd be a peasant to her since you work with your hands."

"Now, Aimee, her mother and father obviously groomed her to be a Southern lady and she'll probably marry into money, so she won't have to work."

A car turned into the approach avenue. "Now who's that?" Luke wondered. "It's not Sunday."

"Speak of the devil, that's old man Crapsey himself," Aimee identified the approaching car. "Probably come back to check on progress on his precious mural."

Their lunch might have gone on quite a bit longer if Elder Crapsey hadn't pulled up in his new Lincoln, rolled down the window, and said, "Y' got a minute, Pastor Luke?"

"Pastor Luke?" gasped Aimee. "You're the new pastor? Here I thought you were a regular guy! Why didn't you tell me?"

"I'll meet you in the office in five minutes, Elder Crapsey," Luke responded to buy some time and privacy with Aimee to explain.

"I should have told you, Aimee. 'Guess I just wanted to be a 'regular guy' to a beautiful girl. Being a pastor tends to inhibit normal conversation, at least at first. Are we still friends?"

"Oh, sure. What the heck? After all, you saved my life. I never knew a pastor who's as good-looking as you and not inclined to be pompous."

"Thank-you, I think," he responded.

"Well, go along into your church, PASTOR Luke. I'll see you around."

"Perhaps I'll see you in church on Sunday?" he asked.

"Not me. I stopped going years ago. 'Course I might be persuaded to give it another shot," and she grinned.

The Elder's urgent business was a dinner invitation tomorrow evening "to meet my daughter." Luke had to ask for a postponement because he was leaving early next morning to pick up his children in Baltimore.

"Perhaps sometime next week," he told Elder Crapsey. Luke remembered Aimee's opinion of Caroline Crapsey and was sure he could wait to meet her.

After Mr. Crapsey had gone, Luke stopped by the mural to thank Lizzie via Aimee for providing lovely lunches, but explaining that he was expected at home today for lunch.

"If you'd like to meet my children, they'll be at the ten o'clock service on Sunday, Aimee," he told her with his best smile.

Without making a commitment about Sunday, Aimee said, "Safe trip, Pastor Luke."

Chapter Three

Luke pulled out early Friday morning to drive to Baltimore, Maryland. He hoped the twins would be fairly well packed up for the return trip Saturday. As he drove along on his three-hundred plus mile journey using the faster Route 81 rather than the more scenic Blue Ridge Highway, his thoughts turned to the past week and Aimee.

"Emily," he addressed his long-dead wife out loud, "I think you would like Aimee. She has that same zest for life I always admired in you. She is full of fun and natural curiosity. Now that I've met some of the townspeople she described to me, I know she is a good judge of character. I can't wait to meet the pharmacist who she says is a member of my congregation. Emily, she's the first woman who's caught my eye since I lost you. Her smile lights up her face, and she's really a talented artist. You don't mind, do you,

Em? I miss you so much, but our children really need a mother…and I need someone.

"I'm very excited about having my own congregation finally. That's what we were aiming for so long ago when I first felt called to become a pastor and we applied to Harvard Divinity School. Then when we discovered we were expecting twins, that went on hold. I don't know what I've done with two premature babies and you suddenly gone if Lydia hadn't come. Somehow, we helped each other through her grief over her husband being killed in that Cincinnati plane crash and my shock over your death and having to provide for the twins.

I remember how every day we'd visit Andy and Mandy in the hospital to hold them and sing to them? You had that wonderful nursery all ready, but Lydia came to take care of the little tykes who had to be fed and changed every three hours night and day.

"Then Lydia volunteered to stay and help me raise Andy and Mandy. She was sort of a young grandmother although really only their aunt. So you saw how I was able to go on to seminary the next year. I have to tell you, Em, our twins were the darlings of Harvard Square. I'm sorry you missed all that.

"They're still a handful, Em—so full of life and curiosity. They are bright like we hoped they'd be. God was good to us. For a while, I was afraid we would lose all three of you. The doctors told me it was 'touch and go'."

Luke drove on in silence mile after mile admiring the mountain scenery. Finally, he pulled off to stretch his legs, did a few calisthenics, refilled his thermos with orange juice, and bought gas. A glance at the map showed him to be a third of the way to his mother's home in Baltimore. He took the tape recorder out of its case and placed it on the seat beside him, then clipped the mike to his tee-shirt. The moral and ethical stories he contributed regularly were published by an ecumenical Sunday school press nationwide together with questions and answers for parents and children. He was currently working on a deadline for five stories by September and he'd fallen behind his schedule during the move. It helped pass the time to dictate them as he sped along. He always child-tested his stories by reading them to the twins. Sometimes he even consulted the twins about how his characters should act. His writing provided some supplementary income, for youth pastors are seldom overpaid.

Seminary had cost quite a bit, and what investments were left, he was saving toward putting the twins through college. At least he had managed to graduate without large debts like many of his classmates. Besides, he enjoyed making up stories. "I must have inherited Grandmother's way with words," he thought as he remembered how she made up stories just for him at bedtime. "Funny how these stories always ended with some pertinent point about how God had intervened or taken care of the major character. Then, she'd hear my prayers, tuck me in, and in no time, it was morning again."

His current story was to parallel the parable of the prodigal son featuring a frightened little runaway boy. The miles whizzed by on the big highway as he automatically drove and dictated. Suddenly, a sign indicated the junction with Route 66 toward Washington, D.C. He shut the tape recorder off since he'd need to pay more attention as traffic increased from many small towns along the elevated highway. The 495 Beltway would let him skirt Washington, D.C. and move on into Maryland and Silver Springs.

"Only forty-some miles to go," he told his road-weary self. "Hope Mother has a good dinner waiting for all of us. Gosh, it'll be good to be with the twins again! This sturdy Volvo always brings us through."

He neared Johns Hopkins University on University Parkway. The family condominium was part of the splendid complex in the Guildford area. Many University-associated couples lived there when they gave up their large homes after children were grown and gone. Luke wheeled into the parking area beneath the complex and identified himself to the attendant. He was assigned a guest parking place.

With his overnight suitcase in hand, Luke took the elevator from the parking garage. The twins were waiting when Luke pressed the buzzer at Number 14. They flung open the door and leaped on their dad.

"Daddy, you should have seen what we saw at the Smithsonian," Andy said.

Amanda added, "We saved some pistachio ice cream for you, Dad."

"Don't I get a kiss?" Luke asked.

"Oh, sure, Dad. We were waiting so long for you!" They took turns hugging and kissing him.

"Now, where are your grandparents?" Luke asked.

"Right here, Son. 'So glad to see you made it. That's a long trip." Luke hugged his father and when his mother appeared from the kitchen, she kissed him and commented, "How tanned and fit you look!"

"That's because I've been planting and tending those rosebushes you sent. What a nice surprise they were, Mother."

"Roses were your grandmother's favorites. Come along. We've already eaten, but we'll keep you company while you eat. How about roast beef and roasted potatoes plus asparagus?"

"It all sounds wonderful," he assured her.

After supper, Luke and the twins went for a fast walk around the complex. When the twins had gone to bed in anticipation of an early start for Loch James, Luke stayed up for coffee with his folks. After he'd thanked them for hosting the children an entire week while he and Lydia moved and got settled, his mother gave him some advice.

"Your children are delightful, Luke, but they need a mother. You know how we loved Emily, but it's high time you found another wife and mother for your family. Andy, of course, can pattern himself after you. In looks, he'll resemble his mother's brothers. But poor Mandy needs a young mother, and it's not fair to Lydia that she has to sacrifice her life. She's entitled to remarry and find some personal happiness.

Mandy, unlike her sleeping brother, was eavesdropping from the cracked open bedroom door. She listened intently for Luke's answer of a new mother.

"Mother, I have just met a lovely young woman, but it's certainly too soon to think about marrying her. Any woman I'd consider would have to get along well with my children."

"You do look well, Luke. I think meeting this woman has lightened your spirit. It warms my heart to hear you laughing again. As the Bible says in Proverbs 17:22, 'A merry heart does good like a medicine.' Tell me about her."

"Aimee—spelled the French way—is vivacious and fun to be with. She's a talented artist who has a home in the mountain above Loch James where she lives with her mother's nanny whose husband is sort of a caretaker. The day I visited 'Painter's Pond' I saw a gorgeous rainbow. It seemed like a sign from Heaven of better days ahead. How the children will enjoy her geese, goats, horses, chickens, and sheepdog! She studied in Paris where her father came from. He also was a painter, but Aimee has grown up in Loch James. She's doing a mural at the church and she didn't even guess I was the new pastor for three days after we met. I felt so young again."

"So how did you meet her?" asked his father.

"You won't believe it, but she literally fell into my arms… from the scaffolding," he added.

"Didn't she hurt herself?" his mother asked.

"She's quite petite, Mother, so I was able to break her fall without either of us getting hurt. Then she had the nerve to be angry with me because she said I caused her to fall. But we had lunch together and ended up friends. The next day it rained and she couldn't paint, so she invited me to see her mountain home."

"Aha, she's after you, son," his father cautioned.

"No, Dad, at that point she still thought I was a landscaper, so she's not after my money."

"So, it was your good looks you inherited from me," said his father and laughed.

"That's what I fell for forty years ago," added his mother, and they all laughed together.

"Well, we'll look forward to meeting this Aimee. Meanwhile, you'd better get some rest ahead of the trip tomorrow. Thanks for lending us Mandy and Andy. They're great kids, but we'll need a couple of days to recover after you leave."

Young Mandy quietly closed the bedroom door, slipped into bed, and dreamed of a wicked stepmother.

Six o'clock the next morning Luke and his parents bundled the drowsy children into the Volvo to begin the trip home. Grandmother had provided a carton of orange juice and a box of doughnuts for a wayside breakfast. There was a hot coffee in a thermos for Luke who'd promised the twins MacDonald's for lunch.

The farewell was lightened by looking forward to a Thanksgiving reunion in Loch James. His parents were eager to see his new church and surroundings. Luke was grateful for quiet time while the twins dozed.

Mandy was the first one to come to. He'd noticed how restlessly she was sleeping.

"Why don't you join me upfront here and we'll let your brother continue to sleep?" he invited Mandy.

"Okay, Dad," and when he slowed over to the side of the road, she climbed over the seat and buckled the passenger side seat belt. It was always a privilege to be upfront as her father's navigator.

"Dad, can I ask you something?"

"What's on your mind, Mandy?"

"I overheard you tell Grandma about a lady painter you met and like to go up to her house. If you marry her, she'll be a stepmother for me and Andy, won't she?"

"Not all stepmothers are ugly and wicked, Mandy, but slow down. I've only known Aimee for a week and I'm not intending to marry anyone. She's just a friend. You'll probably like her. She's said you and Andy can help her paint the sides of the picture—the mural—she's doing on the outside of our church."

"What sort of picture is it, Dad?"

"It's Christ with the children."

"Oh wow! Wait until Andy hears he gets to paint with a real live artist!"

"Do you remember the story about Christ and the children?" he asked her.

"That He loved them?" she asked.

"Yes. Wherever He went He'd gather the children around Him and tell them stories called parables. He even let the parents listen in," Luke explained.

"Did He make them laugh?" she asked.

"Probably. He certainly smiled at human nature, for He loved those who listened to Him. I believe Aimee has painted Jesus with a smile. He also has brown hair and a beard in this mural."

"So the lady's name is Aimee? I sort of like that name," said Mandy.

"She loves animals and she's invited you two to come to her house to meet her geese and other animals."

"What other animals?" asked Mandy.

"Well, she has some retired racehorses that can be ridden, but not raced anymore. She has a sheepdog who is about to have puppies. She'll no doubt be looking for homes for those puppies soon," he added.

"Do you think Aunt Lydia would let us have puppies— one for me and one for Andy?"

"You'll have to ask her," Luke said as he thought, *I walked right into that one, didn't I? Maybe I'll have to get the backyard fenced. Better check with the Session about that.*

Mandy did a little female reasoning to help the puppy cause. "You could even write stories for the Sunday School paper about the puppies," she suggested. "We could train them to do tricks!" Wanting to add weight to her arguments, she leaned over and said loudly, "Andy, you'd like a puppy, wouldn't you? What would you name him?"

Andy was awake in no time at the prospect of a puppy. "I'd call him 'Shep' and we'd get him a collar and a ball… and a bed. He'd need a leash and a water dish…"

Luke groaned.

Mandy added, "I'm going to name mine Aimee 'cause I like that name."

Andy protested. "I won't know whether you're calling me or the dog. Who do you know named Aimee anyway?"

"Dad's friend, the painter."

"What painter?"

Now the fat's in the fire, Luke thought. So Luke repeated what he'd told Mandy about Aimee and how she was going to let them help her with the sides of a mural.

"That's awesome!" Andy said with shining eyes. "Do you 'spose she could give me lessons? I love to paint!"

Luke said, "Andy, remember when you looked up at the sky and saw a rainbow? Well, I saw a rainbow at Aimee's house and she has added a rainbow to the mural."

"I don't know how to paint a rainbow, Dad," he said in a discouraged voice.

"Perhaps you can look at hers and then duplicate it for yourself. That's how some of the greatest painters learned, and you already have watercolors."

Andy cheered up at this prospect. "Aimee told me she sometimes has painting classes on her porch, but I believe they're for grownups. We'll ask her about lessons, though," Luke offered.

"How about we stop for a bite of breakfast and a run around the car? There's a scenic pull-off up ahead and it has bathrooms. Ten minutes and we'll meet at the picnic table for juice and doughnuts."

"I want a chocolate one," Andy specified.

"There are at least two of them," Luke assured him. "Your grandmother knows better than to pack only one of anything."

"When we have our dogs," Mandy continued, "we'll have to walk them when we stop, right Dad?"

"I suspect so," Luke said in a resigned voice, running a hand through his hair. He had a feeling he'd only begun to hear about the puppy matter.

Underway again, Luke decided to begin the twins' orientation. "Let me tell you about our new home," he began. "Each of you will have your own bedroom just as Aunt Lydia and I both have private bedrooms. There are two bathrooms on the second floor. Downstairs, there are living room, dining room, kitchen, half-bath, study, and a glassed-in sun porch for watching T.V.

We have a large yard and Aunt Lydia and I have already planted vegetables..."

"Oh yuck!" came from Andy in the back seat.

Quickly, Luke shifted the emphasis to the peach and apple trees—good for fruit or for CLIMBING," he added for the benefit of the boy in the back. "We even have a grape arbor. If anyone asks, our new address is 64 Lake View Avenue." They repeated it twice. "It is just two blocks from Main Street where there's only one traffic light for the whole town of Loch James."

Mandy said, "A real Hicksville, huh?"

"You will be able to walk to school and stores without having to wait for a ride, Mandy. Or you can ride your bike on the back streets rather than only in the park," Luke replied. "The school has tennis courts, too, Mandy."

"Good. I might even beat you there," Mandy said enthusiastically.

"I haven't met any children yet, but I know there are plenty of youngsters because there is a full Sunday school and youth group at the church. We'll have to buy new school clothes, too, because they don't wear uniforms here."

"Can I wear jeans, Dad?" Mandy asked excitedly.

"We'll find out before school starts in September. You may be two sizes bigger by that time," he said from expensive experience. "We'll find a mall before then. The drugstore," Luke continued, "has an old fashioned soda fountain with great ice cream sodas and banana splits. You sit on red leather stools by the counter. On our way home from church, we can stop for ice cream cones if you like."

"It sounds good to me!" piped up Andy.

The persistent Mandy asked, "Does your new friend Aimee live near us?"

"No, she lives quite aways off up a mountain."

"Mountains?" Mandy echoed. "Like Mount Everest?"

"Not that high," said Luke with a laugh. "You can drive to her place. She has a waterfall and a log home."

"A log cabin," Andy asked, "like in <u>Little House on the Prairie</u>?"

" 'Fraid not, hon. It's made of logs all right, but it's a large, modern home. There's a porch and you can look off for miles into the distance without seeing another person."

"It's a wilderness?"

"Not really. They have electric lights, dishwasher, and T.V., young Daniel Boone. Aimee even has a mammy."

Mandy was obviously picturing Aunt Jemima when she asked, "With a turban and an apron?'

"Lizzie does most of their cooking, but she dresses just like everybody else, Mandy. She makes delicious sugar cookies. She'll be 'Miss Lizzie' to you children. She's elderly and deserves to be treated with proper respect. She actually helped raise Aimee. Lizzie's husband, Clem, keeps the goats."

"How many? Are they pets?" asked Andy.

"You'll just have to wait and see. Clem might even let you help gather eggs from their chickens."

"They must have a farm up there on the mountains," commented Mandy.

Luke changed direction. "Now, when you meet new people, what do you say to them?"

"Hi", ventured Andy.

"Perhaps to another youngster, but to an adult," his father explained, "you should say, 'I'm pleased to meet you, ma'am or sir. If they ask who you are, tell them, 'My father is the new pastor at the Community Church and we live at 64 lake View Avenue. My name is Andrew and my sister is

Amanda. We're twins and eleven years old'. That should get the conversation going. You might politely ask what their names are."

"Gee, we have to learn everybody's name again," grumbled Mandy.

"Just take it one day at a time," he advised her. Tomorrow is our first Sunday, and we won't be able to remember everyone's name right away. Smile even if you don't know the people."

Luke's orientation lesson was cut short when a sign beating a pair of golden arches let them know it was only two miles to MacDonald's. A discussion about menu possibilities broke out between Mandy who wanted a grown-up cheeseburger plus chocolate milk and Andy who had no such pretensions and coveted a toy in a hamburger Happy Meal. Luke was grateful for the playground and planned to order a fish sandwich and coffee for himself. Idly, he wondered what Aimee would have ordered if she'd been with them.

In the late afternoon, Luke sighted an old pickup truck pulled off to the side of the road. Its driver was frantically waving, so Luke slowed down noticing that there were no flashing emergency lights or flares at the scene. "I'm pulling off right ahead of this fellow," Luke told the twins. "You two stay put and keep quiet. Let me handle this." Luke quickly stopped on the shoulder of the road as he'd said he would.

The distraught driver ran up to Luke's Volvo.

Luke rolled down his window. "What's wrong?" he asked.

"I don't know. There's plenty of gas, but I just barely made it off the road after the engine quit. I can't get it started again and the lights don't work."

"Do you have flares or emergency triangles to keep anyone from running into you?" Luke asked.

"No, sir."

Luke reached into the side pocket on his door and offered the man two emergency flares. "Here. Put these in place, then come back and we'll use my cell phone to call for some assistance."

"That's great, mister. Thanks for stopping! Could I also call my wife? She'll be worried 'cause I'm late."

"Sure", Luke agreed.

When the man returned from placing and lighting the flares, his pickup was now clearly visible in the purplish-red light of the flares. "Do you live around here?" asked Luke.

"About ten miles down the road on my farm," he explained. "I can call my brother and he'll come out to help me. He's good at fixing motors."

Luke showed him how to use the cell phone. Before long, his brother Silas was on the way and his wife reassured. Gratefully, the man offered to give Luke a bag of the June apples with which the truck was loaded.

"I'm a new father," the man explained, "and we don't have a lot of cash to spare, but you're more than welcome to some of my apples."

"Why, thank you," Luke accepted. "We'd like some apples, wouldn't we, kids?"

When the man returned with a sack of apples, Luke asked, "How far are we from Loch James?"

"About ten miles," the man answered.

"Do you know the Community Church in Loch James?" asked Luke.

"Sure. My mother goes to it."

"What's her name?" Luke asked curiously.

"Rita Jamison and I am her son, Bob."

"Pleased to meet you, Bob. I'm Pastor Luke Carson and these are my children, Mandy and Andy. Say hello, kids."

"It's OK to talk now, Dad?" asked Mandy.

"Yes, I was just being cautious at first when we stopped," Luke explained.

"Well, Bob, we need to get on down the road. It sounds like your brother will be here shortly. Come to church with your mother sometime. Thanks for the apples."

"Thank you again for your help," Bob said and waved good-bye as Luke carefully pulled onto the highway again.

Mandy asked, "Dad, do you always stop to help people along the road?"

Her father answered," Don't you remember Our Lord's story about the Good Samaritan? Everyone is our neighbor."

"Yes, but Aunt Lydia said not to talk to strangers."

"Why, Daddy? He was a nice man," Andy said.

"This man was a good man, but there are people who rob and hurt people," Luke answered.

"How do you know the difference?" asked Mandy.

"Always be polite, but cautious at first," Luke replied, "until you get to know the people and the situation better. You noticed I did not get out of our car, but I was able to help with flares and the use of my cell phone."

When they pulled into the driveway of the parsonage, Lydia came racing out to meet them. The twins exploded out of the back seat to hug her and receive kisses.

"We've missed you, Aunt Lydia."

"And I've missed both of you, too, she assured the twins.

"Dad was a good Samaritan this afternoon," bragged Andy.

"I'll want to hear all about that at supper," she said with a nod to Luke. "Now help your dad unload the car and come into supper. It's almost ready."

Luke stretched after the long ride. "It was a good trip, Lydia. The twins were really well-behaved, and I can't wait to introduce them to church tomorrow."

Chapter Four

Luke was up early on this, his first Sunday at Loch James Community Church. Lydia had watched him carefully brush off his dark Italian suit and check the part in his hair in the hall mirror.

"Okay handsome, let's get a good breakfast into you before you leave for the church," she commanded. "I've never seen you so nervous before."

"I feel like a young pilot before his solo flight," Luke said. "In a month or so I'll be used to heading my own congregation where the buck stops here instead of just assisting. With God's help, I'll make a good initial impression and begin a fruitful relationship with this congregation today." He polished off his eggs and bacon and gulped down a second cup of coffee, thanked Lydia and kissed her cheek. Then, he began to walk briskly toward the church with his Bible under one arm. He wanted to be early enough to place his sermon notes on the pulpit and be sure there was a glass of water on the shelf underneath. His academic robe hung ready in the closet of his study.

As he neared the entrance of the church, he inspected the recently planted rosebushes. Yes, there were new leaves on all of them, thanks to soaking their roots regularly. He hoped they'd be blooming by the time his parents came to visit. Luke unlocked his study door and sat down for a few quiet moments of prayer. "You know how important today is, Lord. You led me here. Please help me reach the hearts of these people so they'll come to love You more. Amen."

Donning his academics robe, Luke looked himself up and down in the long mirror on the back of his closet door. "I wish Aimee could see me now, a far cry from my gardening self." He grinned ruefully. "Now where did that thought come from? I'd better concentrate on looking over my sermon and remember to smile as Lydia reminded me over breakfast. Then my old homiletics prof emphasized how important eye contact is."

He glanced at his watch when he heard the organist beginning to warm up. It's time for the verger to ring the fifteen-minute bell in the church tower. He went out and placed his sermon notes on the pulpit, was pleased to see that the sexton had remembered the glass of water in case his throat got dry.

Laughing voices sounded from the Choir Room where the choir members were already robing. *"My choir"*, he thought to himself. Soon they'd climb into the choir loft in the back of the sanctuary and the organist would begin the prelude. The twenty-voice choir and magnificent Ruckers organ were features of this church that had helped attract him here. He knew how important good music is to worship.

The ushers with their name tags were busily seating latecomers, but most of the congregation had arrived in time to select their favorite places in the pews. As the organist concluded the prelude, Luke moved to face the congregation. Lydia and the twins were smiling up at him from a front pew. He cleared his throat and spoke into the welcoming silence. "Good morning. We will start our worship service with hymn number 46—'Holy, Holy, Holy'. Please stand."

He smiled up at the choir in the back and the service proceeded according to the bulletin through the Bible readings and prayers. Then, it was sermon do-or-die time. He began by introducing himself with a smile. "My name is Lucas Lee Carson III or "Pastor Luke." My family and I are very pleased to be here in Loch James with you. Let me introduce my family. They're here in the first row. Please stand and turn around. Aunt Lydia Hammond and my eleven-year-old twins, Amanda and Andrew or Mandy and Andy." They bowed to enthusiastic applause and sat down again. "Everyone is new to me, but you all already know one another, so please be sure to tell me your name when you talk to me so that I can learn yours.

"To start with, I was pleased to see so many of you carrying your Bibles when you came in. The Bible is our Christian textbook. The summary of Law is the Ten Commandments and the New Testament is the fulfillment of the law and prophecies of the Old Testament by Christ and his followers. The parables are applicable to our lives, for they deal with human nature which has changed little over time."

Luke went on to liken Bible study to a visit to the beach. Children like to play in the sand and water, then they learn to swim and name shells, and finally they mature into adults who become very knowledgeable about dangers and advantages of the sea. "So we will together be often revisiting familiar Biblical passages, each time gleaming more to apply to our lives as individuals and a congregation. We will pray more, and we will reach out in love more to those around us. Not just our church family, but to the community and places farther away. May God bless and strengthen us as we begin our mutual ministry," he concluded.

Next, he announced the offering and added, "I understand we have some special surprise music about which the choir director wouldn't even tell me." Luke sat down and looked back toward the choir loft.

A woman stood alone stroking a dulcimer softly. Then she began in a low, true voice without trained vibrato or artificial attacking of notes to sing the old mountain lyrics of "Tis a Joy to Be Simple." Luke sat stunned. It was Aimee with her hair loose about her shoulders who was singing so plaintively and beautifully!

Aimee—here in the church! Thank-you God," he thought. *"This makes today complete that she is here with me. How I hope she liked my sermon. May her heart be moved to keep coming."*

At the close of her solo, the congregation rose and everyone sang the Doxology as the ushers came back down the aisles and presented the offering. Pastor Luke reminded the congregation about the coffee hour to follow the service and called for any visitors to introduce themselves. The service closed with the spirited hymn "A Mighty Fortress is Our God." During the last stanza, Luke proceeded up the aisle to be in position at the back to pronounce the benediction and shake hands with people as they exited the sanctuary and moved to the Sunday School Room for coffee hour.

Aimee, from the choir balcony, liked the way Luke strode confidently up the aisle, his shoulders back and singing loudly from his diaphragm in a strong baritone voice. *"A man like that is a natural leader*, she told herself. *I could follow him almost anywhere!*

Most of the congregation chose to stay for coffee and a piece of the special cake welcoming Pastor Luke. Aimee was at the end of the choir who had already taken off their robes. She had on a simple white linen shirtwaist dress with a red belt and high-heeled red sandals. Luke looked her over appreciatively and Aimee blushed as she shook his hand when it was her turn.

"Your singing was beautiful, Aimee," he complimented her. "I hardly recognized you."

She grinned up at him, "Nor I you. We clean up pretty well, don't we?" They laughed together.

Lydia came up just then to remind Luke that the congregation was waiting in the Sunday School Room for him to say grace over the refreshments. "Tell them I'll be right there," he said. "Before you go, Lydia, I'd like you to meet Aimee St. Claire, the artist I told you about."

"I'm VERY pleased to meet you, Aimee," Lydia said. "When I stop the children from eating too much cake, I'd like a chance to visit with you. You are coming in, aren't you?" When Aimee nodded assent, Lydia hurried away.

"Come along, Aimee," Luke said. "You've certainly earned a piece of cake."

As they entered the room, Luke signaled for quiet and said the blessing. Immediately the ladies served cake, punch, and coffee. When everyone had been served, Luke was circulating among his new flock. He complimented the grandmother who had made the fancy cake, then visited briefly at each table.

Lydia made a point of sitting down next to Aimee. "I really love your voice!" Lydia began. "It's so natural and true—like I've heard from children's choir soloists."

"Why, thank you. Luke has told me how much he has depended upon you since his wife died."

"Well, I couldn't leave Luke to raise a set of twins by himself. Besides, I love Andy and Mandy as if they were my own. Speaking of the twins, here they come. Oh, Mandy, you've spilled something on your dress!"

"I'm sorry, Aunt Lydia. I bumped into somebody when my punch cup was full." Then the little blonde continued breathlessly, "I just met Debbie. She's my age, and we'll be in the same grade. Her father is a doctor."

"That's nice, dear. Mandy, this is your father's artist friend, Aimee."

"Oh, you're the one whose dog has puppies!" Mandy said.

Andy came closer having overheard his sister's exclamation. "You're the lady with the dogs? When can we come and see them?"

Aimee smiled at the two eager youngsters who looked so much like Luke. "Well, that's up to your father. Why don't you come over tomorrow morning and watch me paint?"

"Can Debbie come, too?" asked Mandy.

"Sure, but don't wear your good clothes," Aimee warned. *With school out, it'll be a miracle if I didn't have a sizable audience,* Aimee thought. *'Guess I'd better bring along some sketch pads and chalks tomorrow.*

Luke arrived at their table. "I see you've gotten to know my family."

Lydia said, "I'll bet you're tired now, Luke, but you were God's messenger today. Let's head for home, have a good dinner, and you can nap or watch baseball on television."

"That sounds good, Lydia. Care to join us for dinner, Aimee?" he asked.

"Thanks for the invitation, but Mammy and Clem are expecting me."

"Mammy?" asked Mandy.

"Actually, she was my mother's mammy, but keeps house and cooks for me now," Aimee explained. "You'll get to meet her when you come to visit me at Artist's Pond. That's the name of my home up on the mountain."

"Thanks again for making today so memorable with your singing and dulcimer, Aimee," Luke thanked her.

"Actually, Clem made this dulcimer for me."

"Somebody here made your dulcimer?" marveled Mandy.

"Clem is an artist with wood. You'll get to see his instruments and carvings when you come. He is Mammy's husband and does all the outside work."

Andy spoke up. "I'd sure like to meet him."

"All in good time, kids," Luke broke in. "We need to get home to dinner and let Aimee leave to go where she needs to. You'll be able to talk with her again tomorrow. Run along now."

Luke carried the dulcimer out to Aimee's truck for her. "How about coming down in your pony cart tomorrow for the children's sakes?"

"Good idea, Luke. Thank you for making my first church visit in ten years quite enjoyable." She pulled out of the parking lot leaving Luke to ponder the implications that despite her appearance today, Aimee was not a regular church-goer.

The twins set off with their father at nine the next morning to walk the two and a half blocks to the Community Church. Almost as soon as they paused to admire the mural, they heard the clip-clop of hooves on the approach road. Whirling around at the sound, the twins ran out to meet the pony cart and Aimee. How they laughed and shouted in greeting her, delighted with the yellow trap and red leather harness on a small Morgan mare, beige with crème tail and mane. Aimee halted the outfit and let the children climb aboard for the remaining short distance to the church; they greeted Luke with a wide smile.

On such a pleasant day he was feeling very chipper and loving the sight of Aimee with his children. While Luke unbuckled the mare and led her away to the spare lot where he'd seen Aimee tether the horse, Aimee said to the twins: "Okay, these are the rules for being here with me and the mural. You paint only what I say to paint since I am the artist in charge. When you're finished what I've assigned you, you wash your own brushes. I'll show you how. I've also put sketch pads and colored chalks in the cart so you can make your own pictures to take home."

Luke interrupted to tell her he would be back to claim the twins and take them home for lunch.

"How about their coming back to ride home with me between one and two o'clock, Luke? You could pick them up later." The twins nodded hopefully. In a stage whisper, she added, "I understand you promised each of these two a puppy."

"Well," Luke said defensively, "we were talking about your place to pass the time on our journey here. Somehow the subject of dogs and puppies came up, and I mentioned you had some. The kids just took it from there."

Aimee had to grin. "Maybe I could find a puppy or two so as to not make a liar out of you, Pastor Luke." Luke felt himself flushing as he laughed at himself. "You're certain your kids wouldn't each like a four-legged kid?" she teased.

"No, I'm afraid Lydia would leave home at that point."

"Your aunt is a very kind and gentle person, Luke. You're really lucky to have her taking care of your home and children."

"I prefer to believe that Lydia was a Godsend for my children," Luke replied, and he left heading for a morning of mail and appointments in his study at the church.

Aimee was working on one of the children pictured at the feet of Christ in the mural. She'd assigned Mandy to paint some background near the base of the mural, and Andy was stroking in some blades of grass near rocks on the other end.

"You know," Mandy pointed out after about half an hour of diligent painting, "that Christ up there looks a lot like Dad if he had a beard."

"Yes, your father is tall and has brown hair and eyes, too," Aimee agreed and went on to explain, "No one really knows what Christ looked like. Folks didn't have cameras back then, and Jesus was too poor to pay for someone to paint his portrait."

Andy was paying close attention now, looking up at the figure of Christ. "He sure has a happy smile!"

Aimee said, "I painted it that way because I believe Jesus loved children and enjoyed being with them. What do you think?"

"I guess so," Andy said. "We always sang 'Jesus Loves Me' when I was a little kid in Sunday school."

"Oh, you!" laughed Aimee and made a playful swipe at him with her paintbrush. "You're practically an old man now, aren't you?"

"Maybe Dad should grow a beard," persistent Mandy suggested. "Then he and Christ would really look alike!"

"Why don't you suggest that to him?" said Aimee with a mischievous grin. After all, she owed him one for those promised puppies.

The rest of the morning passed swiftly. Andy had three pictures to carry home with him, Mandy had one picture, and Aimee had had at least six children helping her at various times. Despite supervising so many, she had progressed to Christ's arms held wide to encompass several children. As lunchtime decimated her crew, Aimee breathed a sigh of relief. She considered the face of Christ intently. Had she subconsciously copied Luke's features? As Mandy had pointed out, there was a decided resemblance.

I didn't intend to do that! Whew...I think I'd better change the shape of the nose slightly and make his hair longer or Luke might notice, too. But that smile I'll keep. It is very like the one Luke gave me when I finished my solo. It made me feel so cherished.

Tomorrow I'll sketch in the rainbow. My father used to paint rainbows. I'll study some of his paintings tonight to check on the shadings.

She quickly ate the lunch she'd brought, drank an extra cup of cold lemonade, and hurried to make the slight changes to Christ's face before Luke and the children returned. After all, Mandy was not one to keep thoughts to herself, so no doubt the resemblance would have come up over lunch.

Sure enough, when Luke returned at one-thirty with the twins all atwitter about visiting Poet's Pond, Aimee saw Luke studying the face of Jesus in the mural. "Something wrong?" she asked.

"No, but I can't see where Mandy got the idea that you'd used my face for Christ's. I would have been flattered, but it would have been a mistake. Yes, Christ was a man, but there should also be something ethereal about him."

"You don't see yourself as particularly ethereal?" she asked.

Luke knew that his thoughts about Aimee were anything but ethereal. Very defensively, he said, "Woman, I am the pastor here and don't you forget it!"

Aimee returned a mock salute and said, "Yes, Sir!" They both laughed. "What time will you be coming for the twins?"

"Will four-thirty be all right? We don't want to keep Lydia's supper waiting."

"Good. I'll get Dolly hitched up again and we'll be on our way."

"Aimee," he asked, "could you go by side streets until you're out of town? That way, there'll be less traffic and commotion for you and the children."

Aimee was not used to being given orders, but it was endearing that Luke was trying to keep them safe. "We'll be careful," she assured him. *Guess I'd better not tell him that Mandy asked to take the reins once we get out of town,* she decided.

Andy was content to sit in the back with the supplies and watch the mountain vistas. Mandy sat next to Aimee and never stopped asking questions on the way. Aimee answered quite a few of them by saying, "You'll see when we get there." She did take the back streets until they were past the center of town. As they went under the highway overpass, Andy let out a loud whistle, marveling at the sound of the huge trucks passing overhead.

Soon they began to climb upward. Mandy did get to take the reins and learned quickly how to guide the horse with them. She even copied Aimee's clicking noises to increase the pace. Dolly, the mare, pricked up her ears and dutifully went along. As the road became more narrow and steep, Aimee took over the reins again. Mandy leaned over to whisper to Andy, "Don't you tell Dad I was driving. He said we have to wait until we are sixteen."

"That was for cars, doofus," Andy responded, "but I can keep a secret."

Aimee said, "Maybe you'd like to learn to drive a horse next time, Andy."

"I'll think about it," replied Andy, the artistic introvert.

When they came abreast of the pasture containing both horses and sheep, the twins were entranced by the playful, black-faced lambs gamboling about.

"Ooh, can we stop and pet them?" begged Mandy.

"Let's go on up to the house. Then Clem can show you the animals," Aimee replied. "We're nearly there."

"Those horses look really big and beautiful," commented Andy.

"They're retired thoroughbred racing horses," Aimee explained.

"Why do you keep them if they don't race anymore?" asked Mandy.

"These horses have earned a great deal of money for their owners, and now their grateful owners pay to have them taken care of in retirement. If you'd like, you can even ride them at an easy pace, but no more racing for them."

"Today? Could we ride them today?" pressed Mandy.

"Today, you're just getting to know your way around here. Besides, they've already been exercised today by some of our teenaged neighbors. These horses only need mild exercising to maintain their health," Aimee said.

She turned the cart into the house lane, and Clem came out of the barn to welcome them. After introductions, Clem took the mare's halter to walk her into the barn for unharnessing. The twins followed him like a pied piper while Aimee turned to go toward the house. "Clem," she requested with a smile, "you'll show Andy and Mandy the animals, won't you? Then please bring them back to the house for refreshments."

"Sure will, Miss Aimee." Clem let the twins push the cart into the corner of the barn. Then they watched with fascination as Clem turned Dolly into her stall. Mandy asked to pet her nose and tell her she was a good girl. Then Clem let Andy give Dolly some oats to supplement her hay.

"Did you see our geese as you pulled up?" Clem asked.

"Yes," Mandy said excitedly. "They followed us up the drive. They're sure noisy!" Clem led the twins out the back door of the barn and toward an enclosure where there were six goats. "Five of these are nanny goats," Clem explained, "but that fellow on top of the shed is our billy goat."

"What's he doing up there?" asked Andy.

"He's playing he's the king of the castle," Clem said jokingly. "You know why we keep these goats?"

Mandy chimed in. "Cause they're pretty."

"No, it's not their good looks," Clem responded. "We milk them."

Mandy looks mystified. "I thought only cows were milked."

"Cows don't give goats' milk and that's what we make our cheese out of," said Clem.

Andy asked, "The square kind like we make our grilled cheese sandwiches from?"

"I doubt you make sandwiches of feta cheese," Clem answered. "When we go back through the barn, I'll give you each a small sample of our cheese."

Andy spoke up. "Do you give puppies goats' milk? Where do you keep the puppies?"

Clem smiled. "I take it you'd like to see the puppies?" Both children nodded enthusiastically. "Well, we have six in this litter, and their mother is very busy what with feeding and washing them."

"What kind are they?" asked Mandy.

"They're Shelties—good sheep herding dogs when they're trained." Clem led them to an empty stall in the far corner of the barn. There on the bed of hay was Duchess with her eight-week-old puppies climbing over her and Duke guarding them.

"Oh, aren't they cute! Can I hold them?" Mandy asked. "How do I pick one up? They're so little."

Clem kept the twins back. "Let me take Duke outside and tie him up. He's terribly protective and might misunderstand your handling of his offspring." When Clem returned, he petted Duchess and praised her, admiring her babies. She relaxed under the special attention, and Clem let each child choose one puppy to hold gently.

"He likes me," claimed Mandy as her puppy snuggled into her shoulder. "What pretty little ears he has."

Andy said, "Mine is sleeping and doesn't want to open his eyes."

"Better put them down carefully before you worry their mother," Clem instructed. "They're too young to leave her. In a few weeks when you come again, they'll be playing all over the yard. When Duke arrived, he was a playful puppy and just look at him now. He's great at herding sheep and is a proud father."

"So how soon will you be looking for homes for the puppies?" Mandy asked eagerly.

"Ten to twelve weeks, I expect, but Miss Aimee's had quite a few calls from people wanting one. She plans to keep one for herself, of course. Why?"

"My dad said we could each have a puppy if Aimee would let us," Mandy insisted.

"Well, that's up to Miss Aimee. Why don't we go on up to the house now for some refreshments and you can talk to her about it?"

On the way, Mandy whispered to Andy, "Do you want the little sleepy one?" Without waiting for an answer, she continued. "I want the one I was holding. He licked my chin, so I know he likes me."

"Well, I like the sleepy one. He's not as noisy as the one you held," said Andy.

As they climbed the steps, crossed the porch, and entered the house, they could smell the pungent odor of freshly baked ginger snaps. "Come, children, and meet my nanny. She's getting out our refreshments," said Aimee.

Lizzie smiled at the children. "My, my, you do look like your daddy! Wash hands there at the sink, then come and sit around the table. Do you like root beer? I made it myself."

"Okay" Mandy agreed. As Lizzie poured two glasses, they heard Luke pull up in the driveway and honk. Aimee went to the door and waved him to come in for a share of the refreshments. Luke had come a bit early, anxious to see Aimee and hoping the twins liked Artist's Pond as much as he did.

As Luke brushed by Aimee, he felt almost an electric charge. She quickly looked up at him, and he realized she had also felt the strong vibrations between them.

Mandy broke the moment by calling to him. "Daddy, I got to hold my puppy!" she said.

Luke felt himself flushing and somehow needing to explain his daughter's comment. "You'll have to forgive Mandy. She's very impulsive." Turning to Mandy, he cautioned her, "All puppies are cute. I think it's premature to set your heart on a particular one, Mandy. We'll visit several times and it's up to Aimee which puppies she'll let you take home." Changing the subject, he commented on the delicious root beer and cookies. "Now. Let's not eat enough to spoil our suppers."

Andy asked quietly, "I hope we can come again soon, please. I'd like to see your waterfall Dad told us about."

"And I'll be glad to show you another time," Aimee said as she ruffled his hair. *What an adorable little boy,* she thought to herself. "I'll be working on the mural for several more weeks. Maybe you can come again to help me," she proposed.

"Well, I'm starting tennis lessons next week," said Mandy.

"I'll come and help you, Aimee," volunteered Andy.

"Good boy," she said. "I'll see you tomorrow morning then."

"C'mon, kids, we've got to get moving," Luke ordered.

"Kids' is it?" laughed Clem. "They got done looking at the goats."

"It's a figure of speech," laughed Luke, "but they're as active as little goats."

"Mandy, Andy, here are the samples of feta cheese I promised you," Clem said as he gave each of them a small, white square.

Mandy reacted immediately to the strange taste. "That doesn't taste like cheese to me! You take the rest," and she offered it to her father. Andy quietly surrendered what was left of his sample, too.

"Feta cheese is good in salads," Luke assured them, but I suppose you consider that an adult thing. I'm sure your

Aunt Lydia likes feta cheese just fine." The children headed for the car.

Luke paused long enough to thank Clem and Lizzie for their hospitality, and then turned to Aimee. "Thanks again, Aimee. I'll see you tomorrow."

On the way home, Mandy commented, "Aimee seems awful nice, but she'd probably change if she were our stepmother."

"Why?" asked a puzzled Luke.

"'Cause all stepmothers are mean," replied his daughter.

Andy, who already loved Aimee, defended her. "Well, I thought she was really nice…and pretty. I'd like to have her as my stepmother."

"How did this stepmother thing get started?" Luke asked.

"Well," said Mandy, "I heard you talking with Grandma…"

The light dawned for Luke. "Oh, Mother's always trying to fix me up with a woman who'll be your stepmother. Don't worry about it. Tell me how you liked the ride up the mountain in the pony cart," he quickly changed the subject.

"It was awesome, Dad!" Mandy and Andy agreed.

Chapter Five

Pastor Luke looked out over his congregation, bemused by the unusually informal attire—even shorts—since it was a church picnic day. He had inherited this tradition and been advised that he was to be a pitcher of one of the teams at the mixed softball game following the service.

Dr. Stewart was pitching for the opposing team composed mainly of choir members. This week Luke had quietly rounded up the able-bodied leftovers including the older members of the Youth Group augmented by Aimee as a shortstop and a couple of college kids home for the summer who could catch and hit creditably. He had been practicing with Mandy, and the non-member college kids had been lured by promises of a fantastic feed at the picnic prior to the game!

Luke had recruited Aimee on his last visit to pick up Andy at her home after a carving lesson with Clem. "I don't suppose you play softball," he'd said wistfully. "My side is short of players for next Sunday."

"I was a good shortstop for the high school girls' softball team. It's been a while, but it probably would come back to me. Of course, you'd have to put up with my yelling encouragement all the time. I'm not a strong, silent type."

Luke laughed. "I had noticed that. Well, if you're game, we'll have a single practice on Saturday afternoon at the high school at two p.m. to help us function as a team. They tell me the church provides red and blue jerseys, so I'll pass those out at the practice. We have a good supply of balls and bats, so just bring yourself and your favorite glove."

"Okay coach," Aimee said with a grin. She wondered how good a player the preacher would be, but it was another chance to spend time near him and get to know Luke better.

By Sunday, Luke was stiff from the practice but quite encouraged about his team's chances of putting on a good show. He was not as pleased about the obvious interest shown by two of the college boys in his vivacious and pretty shortstop. Win or lose, the game and picnic would be over by late afternoon.

Luke remembered to announce that the picnic would replace the customary coffee hour and urged everyone to attend. "In addition", he added, "It is high time another team gave the choir's team some real competition. Both teams will need good cheering sections, and I'm sure there'll be enough food and soft drinks to go around."

Cheers and clapping followed this announcement. The organist struck up "Stand Up, Stand Up for Jesus" for the closing hymn.

Luke stripped off his academic gown to reveal white tennis shorts and a tee-shirt bearing HARVARD across front and back. He changed into tennis shoes and a baseball cap. Now he was ready.

The women of the church under Millie Stewart's able coordination had outdone themselves. On long tables covered with checkered cloths were meat and cheese, home baked rolls, three kinds of baked beans, several varieties of potato salad, pickles, deviled eggs, green and jello salads for those watching their waistlines, and for dessert---pies, and cakes for every taste. There'd be ice cream after the game. It looked like a feast for a hundred although only seventy-some had come.

Everyone had brought their folding chairs and tables, some with umbrellas, so the church lawn looked like a small fairground. Several boom boxes blared with raucous music from the corner where some unattached teenagers had gathered, much to the annoyance of a few of the older members. One of these was ninety-year-old Roberta Snodgrass who was too feeble to make services regularly, but who always attended picnics and funerals. Her sixty-year-old leghorn hat was her distinguishing trademark. She was holding court with several of her female cronies, all of them frowning and exclaiming at the attire and antics of the younger set.

Luke, in circulating among the tables, approached this group and spoke with them. "Glad to see you, Miss Snodgrass," he said politely.

"How do you do?" she responded. "When are you coming to visit me? I understand you've called on just about everyone else in the congregation."

Luke merely grinned having been warned about her acid tongue. "I'll call and set an appointment this coming week," he promised. "I understand you've never missed a church picnic in the last thirty years."

Flattered, Miss Snodgrass unbent a bit and said, "We're going to cheer for your team, Reverend. Who is the pretty young girl in your red team jersey? I don't recognize her."

"That's Aimee St. Clair, my shortstop. You must have known her mother and father. Of course, she has been away studying art in Paris."

"Yes, now I recognize her. She looks like her mother years ago, but she talks with her hands like her father used to." Changing the topic, Miss Snodgrass added, "I understand you're not married, Pastor."

"I'm a widower with two children, but their Aunt Lydia cares for them and is my hostess," Luke explained.

"Well, we have a number of fine young women who'd make you a dandy pastor's wife," the intrepid Miss Snodgrass suggested.

Luke demurred. "When I come to see you, we can discuss this further." As he moved away quickly, he felt himself turning red. *I know age has its privileges, but minding my personal business is surely close to the limits,* he thought. *But she's not saying anything others haven't told me already— family, friends, and now even members of the congregation.*

Lydia was setting their family table when Mandy came along with Aimee. "Aimee can sit with us to eat, can't she?" Mandy demanded. "She's here all by herself."

"Of course she may. But suppose you find your father quickly and tell him we need him to say grace so everybody can start through the food lines."

Mandy looked around and spotted Luke just coming out of the church's back door near his study. He was carrying a megaphone. "Daddy", she shouted. "It's time for the blessing. We're starved!"

A number of people laughed in agreement, and Luke picked up his pace. "Let us pray!" he announced to quiet the crowd. In short order, silence fell, and the food and fellowship were blessed. He reminded his people to invite any single folk to eat with a family and that the softball game would begin at two p. m. on the church's softball field.

When Luke with his plate of careful selections found the family table, he was delighted to see Aimee and the twins already eating while Lydia dispensed cold drinks from their cooler.

"I hope you don't mind, Luke," Aimee said, "but Mandy dragged me over to sit with your family."

"Welcome, welcome," he said enthusiastically.

"What a nice turnout on a perfect day," Aimee enthused.

Mandy joined the conversation. "Did all these people come to see the ball game, Dad?"

"These are mainly church families and I understand that the food is always excellent, Mandy. The ball game is additional fun whether they're playing or watching."

Aimee said, "I remember our picnics and ball games when I was your age, Mandy. I could hardly wait until I was old enough to play."

"How old do you have to be?" Mandy asked stretching as tall as she could.

"Older than you, darling—probably high school anyway."

"Oh, shucks! That's years away!"

Andy spoke up. "I'm the water boy this year. I get to carry cold drinks for the players and towels for when their team is off the field."

"Oh yeah? Who says?" Mandy demanded.

"Doc Stewart said I could do it for both teams."

"Rats!" responded Mandy who hated to be bested at anything.

Aunt Lydia moved to spread oil on troubled waters. "Perhaps you'd like to help me pass out the ice cream bars after the ball game, Mandy."

"Okay!" Mandy agreed. "See, smart aleck, I've got a job, too!" They both moved off to make choices at the dessert table.

"Do you want to warm up your arm, Coach?" Aimee asked since she and Luke were eating lightly ahead of the game.

"That sounds good. In fact, I'm sort of stiff all over after the practice yesterday," he confessed. "Unlike you, I'm not used to a lot of physical exercises. You ride while my time as an athlete is an occasional tennis game with my daughter."

"Maybe you should take up jogging or riding to keep in shape. There are lots of good trails around here," Aimee suggested. "I like to jog early most mornings. Why don't you try it? We could meet at sunup and run before breakfast. That shouldn't interfere with anything you have scheduled."

The idea of often joining Aimee for jogging on her end of town, probably on the reasonably level bicycle path between the town and Lake James, appealed to him. They'd be alone away from the church and their families. "Yes," he agreed. "Let's start tomorrow. When and where shall we meet?"

"How about six fifteen a.m. sharp at the trailhead parking lot?" Aimee suggested.

"You're on!" he agreed. "Now let's lob a few easy throws to warm us both up. Game time is in fifteen minutes."

The two captains met with the referee, Coach "Red" Polinsky from the high school who was a neutral non-member of the congregation and friends with all the Youth Group members. Doc Stewart's team with its choir members and a couple of athletic relatives took the field first.

"Doc" was a pretty fair pitcher and the opposition's first player, Luke's catcher, struck out. That brought Luke up to bat as his team's pitcher. He did a couple of ferocious practice swings. Then he bunted and sprinted to first base while the surprised pitcher had to run to field the bunt and tardily throw it to the first baseman. The congregation in the stands clapped and shouted their approval. Luke smiled and waved his cap at them.

The basemen managed single hits which brought Luke in, and the score at the end of the first inning after both teams had been up stood tied at two to two. There was a shock among Doc's team members who were used to dominating the annual softball game. "We've got to knuckle down here," Doc told his team as they resumed the field. "We've got some real competition this year! Those college kids are good, Pastor Luke is no slouch, and that cute Aimee really keeps them on their toes with her cheering on comments.

Doc pitched over his head—fast, cunning pitches which no one could seem to hit. The top of the third inning passed quickly with three outs and no runs. Now it was the Pastor' time in the field, and the stands were full of cheering fans.

Never in recent memory had the softball game been this thrilling! Luke wound up and pitched a straight, hard ball with which the batter connected.

"I'll get it!" shouted Aimee. But Luke backed up quickly to field the oncoming hard hit. Suddenly he backed into Aimee, knocking her flat and almost stepping on her. Somehow he managed to hang onto the ball for an out.

"Mon Dieu," Aimee protested. "I told you I had it!" As she spoke, she was holding her face and blood was streaming from her nose.

"Oh, Aimee, I'm sorry. Let me help you up!" Luke said. He asked for a time out while he assisted her to the bench where Doc Stewart already waited with some ice. Andy as a water boy held the bucket and towels for Doc. "Is she going to be all right?" asked Andy, dismayed by all the blood.

"Probably," reassured Doc, "but I'll check her over to be sure your father didn't cause her anything more than a nosebleed and possible back eye."

A black eye!" exclaimed Mandy coming just then. "Wow! Dad really hit her, didn't he?"

Luke turned pale as he realized how hard he'd hit Aimee. She looked so small there on the ground, and he felt like an awkward giant next to her.

"Are you listening?" sputtered Aimee angrily. "I called for that ball. What were you doing in my space?"

Doc said, "I think she's going to live, guys, Stand back and give her some room." He had Aimee hold the improvised towel ice-pack on her nose and wiped the rest of her face off. "It looks worse than it really is, but you better stay on the bench for the remainder of the game, Aimee."

That brought another howl from her. "Now look what you've done, Luke! You're liable to lose with me out of the game!"

"I'll shift Peter over from the infield," Luke said.

"I bet you'll let him field anything he calls for," she said bitterly.

"Oh, Aimee, please. I didn't mean to hurt you. I was just excited…"

"And didn't think I could handle it," Aimee finished his thoughts for him.

Torn between smoothing things over with Aimee and getting the game underway again, Luke ordered, "Mandy, you stay with Aimee and keep her supplied with ice, maybe a popsicle or two. I've got to get back in the field. I'm really sorry, Aimee."

"Humph!" was her only response.

"I'll take good care of her," Mandy assured him, and the game resumed.

It was nip and tuck the entire nine innings. First, one team would forge ahead and then the other. Finally Doc and the choir won, but only by one run.

Everyone enjoyed the postgame ice cream, and Aimee had gotten over her anger. It would take a bit longer for her nose and left eye to lose their puffiness. However, so many sympathetic fans had come around she felt she had celebrity status. By the time Luke caught up with her, she only admonished him, "Don't you ever do that again!"

He was so relieved at her forgiveness that he dared to ask, "Will you be up to jogging tomorrow?" Aimee smiled and they agreed to meet privately early the next morning in the prearranged place.

Chapter Six

For five mornings last week, Aimee and Luke had met to jog together. Each morning he'd apologized again and inspected her nose and eye which steadily improved. They'd developed some comradeship on the trail. It's hard to be formal when dressed in running shorts and sweatbands. Aimee, although petite, had a runner's body. She looked with her ponytail like a teenager. Luke had to admit that his physique had firmed somewhat and he could go longer between rest stops.

On this Monday morning, Luke was especially eager to meet Aimee and show her the Richmond newspaper article and picture of her mural, "The Smiling Christ with Children." It had appeared in the colored art section with a very favorable review by the art critic. It hailed her for bringing European art techniques to Virginia and urged readers to attend the formal dedication of the mural of the

Fourth of July. Both the governor and local mayor were to speak after the usual county July 4th parade.

Aimee smiled at Luke as she arrived. "Aren't you going to do your stretches?" she asked.

"First, I want to show you something nice."

"Oh, what?" asked Aimee. Luke unfolded the front page of the art section of the RICHMOND EXAMINOR which displayed a picture of her mural.

"Mon Dieu!" marveled Aimee. "When the writer and photographer were here, I had no idea my mural would rate a feature! Read it to me."

Luke did so, and Aimee hugged him spontaneously when he finished.

"Can I have this to show Lizzie and Clem—then put it in my scrapbook?"

"The newspaper will send you a complimentary copy, but I bought five copies so the twins and church would have copies. Probably the church's copy will even get framed."

"That was nice of the critic to mention my father, too."

"Well, you're part of an artistic heritage in Virginia, Aimee." I liked his mentioning your French training. There aren't very many murals in this part of the country."

"Well there are about to be two more shortly in Roanoke—the Baptist and Episcopalian churches have called. That's too far to commute daily, so I'll only be home on weekends in late July and August."

By this time they were jogging along side by side. "I'll miss you and these mornings," Luke said in a crestfallen voice. "I've come to enjoy starting the day with you."

"Thank you, Luke. I'll miss them too, but it'll only be a month to six weeks for these Roanoke murals. Then we can resume jogging."

"I think the fall must be gorgeous here—the colors of the changing leaves must present a pretty sight," Luke said. "We'll certainly want to be jogging by then."

"Oh, sure," agreed Aimee. "Right now I'm thinking about the 4th of July. I have to get an appropriate dress for the dedication. How about white—like the angels?"

"With your dark hair and eyes, you look good in white. I'll never forget looking back at the choir loft on my first Sunday here watching you as you played and sang your solo." He looked so intently at her as he said this that Aimee blushed at his praise.

Then, changing the subject to something more neutral, she asked, "Do you suppose the church would be willing to produce a brochure for everyone attending the dedication?"

"I'm sure they will," Luke responded. "The congregation is very proud of the mural, and the senior elder has been delighted to see the mural completed in memory of his wife. A brochure could be used later for visitors, too. After all, the newspaper article mentioned the mural as another attraction for area tourists."

Already there was the sound of firecrackers this 4th of July. Units were lining up behind Main Street to march down to the new waystation on the Blue Ridge Trail donated by coal magnate Jackson Montgomery. He had arrived by limousine the previous evening and headed out to his mansion on the shore of Loch James. Several times a year he would descend on the town, usually with a motorcade of attendants and friends—"back to my roots" as Monty liked to say.

Aunt Lydia was as eager and nervous as the twins. Knowing Jackson Montgomery, her old college flame was in town where she might run into him-- she had splurged on a new dress and hat. She had also done her makeup. The twins were astonished.

"Aunt Lydia, you're beautiful today," admired Mandy. "Did you get all dressed up 'cause we're going to see the governor?"

Luke laughed, "Not the governor, Mandy. The gentleman your Aunt Lydia knows could buy and sell the governor several times over."

How much does a governor cost?" asked Andy intrigued by his father's remark. The grownups laughed, easing the tension.

"Well, it's said that every man has his price," his father explained evading a more specific answer. "Your Aunt Lydia used to date Jackson Montgomery over thirty years ago when they were in college, so she's nervous about meeting him again."

"She looks beautiful, Dad. Do you think they'll recognize each other after all that time?" asked Mandy.

"I think so, but I don't know him," Luke said.

"Well, I'm hoping he will remember," said Lydia. "He went away to war and that ended our romance. Well, let's get going. We don't want to miss the parade. Your father has a reserved seat with the dignitaries on the reviewing stand, but we are in the grandstand across from there. Doctor and Millie Stewart said they'd save us three places, but we'd better not keep them waiting."

Sure enough, Doc stood up and waved as soon as Lydia and the twins approached the grandstand. They climbed about halfway up and sat directly opposite the reviewing stand. The twins waved at their father, and Luke waved back at them.

"That your family, Pastor?" asked a deep voice behind Luke. He turned to find a tall gentleman with iron-gray hair, piercing blue eyes, a deep tan, and dressed in a white linen suit with a patterned silk tie.

"I am 'Monty' Montgomery, Pastor, and I've been hearing good things about you."

"Thank you, Mr. Montgomery. It's a pleasure to meet you on this momentous occasion," said Luke.

"Call me 'Monty'. Everybody else calls me that."

"And my parishioners call me 'Pastor Luke.'"

"You have two children?"

"Yes, eleven year old twins. My Aunt Lydia, who's sitting with them, claims she went to school with you."

Monty looked quickly at Luke's family again. "My God, it's Lydia Lee. I'd know her anywhere!" he exclaimed.

"That was her maiden name, but she's Lydia Hammond now," Luke explained.

"So she's married," Monty said with a disappointment in his tone.

"No, she's a widow and is helping me raise my children since their mother died."

Monty cheered up immediately. He was staring at the lovely woman who was returning his gaze. "Hey, Lee," he shouted.

Lydia smiled and waved back at him. Mandy said, "You're getting red, Aunt Lydia."

"Well, it's a hot day, child," Lydia answered quickly, not taking her eyes off the man across from her. *He's still a handsome man—slim with broad shoulders*, Lydia thought as her heart raced. *I used to love to dance with him. The only change I see is that his hair has turned gray, but it's still thick and wavy. Look at that tan! I bet he plays golf or tennis a lot. They say he's very wealthy, but then he came from a rich family. I was at William and Mary on an academic scholarship. He was a big football hero and I was surprised he even noticed me, a reporter for the college paper. But the Korean War changed so much. We went our separate ways. There, he's sitting down. It's almost time for the parade to begin.*

Lydia's attention came back to her two young charges. Millie, sitting next to Lydia, noticed the interchange between Jackson Montgomery and her.

"You know Jackson Montgomery?" Millie asked.

"Yes, we were friends in college," Lydia explained. "I haven't seen him since, but he's still a handsome man."

Millie laughed and added, "Yes, I used to tell Doc when we were dating that he was the second most handsome man in the county. Jackson Montgomery was my number one choice except he was older and rarely here."

A moment later, a young man crossed the street and climbed the grandstand aisle. "Mrs. Hammond?" he inquired as he stopped beside Andy.

"Yes," answered Lydia.

"I have a message for you," and he handed her a note. Then he waited for a reply. Quickly, she unfolded the note and read its contents:

Dear Lee,

How wonderful to see you again. Will you please come to my home for lunch with the governor after the mural dedication? Your nephew says he'll take care of the twins so you can attend. We have much catching up to do, and I'd like to introduce you to my daughter.

Monty

Lydia smiled at the sender across the street and told the messenger, "Please tell Mr. Montgomery that I accept." Thank God, I'm wearing my new outfit, she thought to herself.

Mille was watching curiously, so Lydia could not resist sharing this fascinating new development. "I'm sorry, Millie, but that message was an invitation for lunch with the governor at Monty's home. He even has arranged for the twins to go with Luke to your picnic after the mural dedication so I'll be free to go." Lydia was flushed with excitement.

"Don't worry about missing our picnic," Millie responded. "You can tell me all about the occasion and Monty's house later." They settled down to watch the parade.

The bands played, the marchers went by, floats slowly passed, and at least six hiking clubs were represented in addition to the usual scouts and 4-H groups plus fraternal orders. All corners of the country had thrown in to greet the governor and millionaire with proper pomp and circumstance.

As the last unit was reviewed, it was announced by the mayor that the ribbon-cutting ceremony for the new waystation would begin in fifteen minutes. All were invited and please don't forget the dedication of the Community Church's mural at noon sharp.

The long limousine pulled up to transport the governor, mayor, and Mr. Montgomery to the waystation ceremony. The folks in the grandstand scrambled down to their cars to follow in the procession. Lydia and the twins retrieved Luke's blue Volvo and headed out toward the new trail waystation.

***

Aimee was waiting nervously for people to arrive for the noon dedication of her mural. *Here comes Lionel Crapsey and daughter Caroline all dressed up,* observed Aimee to herself. *Caroline always was something of a clotheshorse. At school dances, she always had to be the belle of the ball with designer fashions. She and her mother would fly to New York City weeks in advance of the dance. No one would know ahead of time what color or style her dress was to be so she could make a grand entrance.*

Then, when she went off to Sweetbriar, she really leaned into the party scene. She and her sky-blue Cadillac convertible were very popular. They tell me she majored in fine arts— photography in particular. Her slim, blonde good looks made her a fabulous model, and she learned how to stress her best features.

She was always careful to preserve her pale skin with sunscreen and hats. If her mother had had her way, Carolyn would have carried a parasol!

"Hi, Mr. Crapsey and Caroline," greeted Aimee. "It's a big day, isn't it?"

"Aimee, you've done nice work on this mural. Our church and my family are very pleased," Mr. Crapsey said. "I see by the newspaper that you've contracted for two more murals on churches in Roanoke."

"That's right," Aimee confirmed.

"You'll have to stay there to do them, won't you?" Caroline asked, not concealing her satisfaction that her rival would be out of town and range of Pastor Luke on whom she had desires. *Maybe Mrs. Carson, his aunt, might stay on to take care of those bratty kids,* she thought to herself. *I'm just not good with kids, but I sure like Pastor Luke. He's so handsome, and we'd make such a perfect couple. Father would approve of Pastor Luke's becoming a part of our family. Besides, in a few years, the twins could be sent off to prep schools.* Yes indeed, with Aimee out of the way. Caroline determined to definitely launch a concerted effort to attract Pastor Luke's interest.

"Of course, I'll be back here on weekends," Aimee assured Caroline.

Just then Lizzie and Clem came over to congratulate Aimee and exclaim over details of the mural with considerable pride in her accomplishment.

"You even painted in a rainbow like your father used to," Clem said.

Lizzie looked up and commented, "My Lord, that smile on Christ's face looks very familiar, Aimee!"

"Ssh," Aimee warned with a finger against her lips. "I didn't mean to copy Luke's face, but when Mandy recognized her father, I quickly changed the shape of the nose and color of his hair before Luke saw it. Swear you won't tell anybody?"

"All right, but better guard your heart, girl," Lizzie warned.

Caroline, standing beside her father to welcome friends and church members, was still mulling over the fact that Aimee would be coming home weekends. *Rats, I knew it was too good to be true—that Aimee would be away for two months! What does Luke see in that paint-splattered farm girl? Oh, joy…here comes Pastor Luke,* and his actual presence drove everything else from Caroline's mind.

Jackson Montgomery's limo pulled up and the governor walked over to pose in front of the mural for the photographers. He assured reporters he'd be available for a press conference with the artist immediately following the brief dedication ceremony.

Monty joined Aunt Lydia and met the twins while Luke waited with the governor and donor to provide a blessing on the new religious mural. Recordings of favorite hymns played while the crowd assembled. Three rows of chairs were provided for the elderly, but everyone else stood for the ceremony on the church lawn.

At noon sharp, Pastor Luke stepped up to the small, temporary podium and welcomed the crowd. He introduced the donor, Elder Crapsey, who'd provided it as a way to memorize his wife, a long-time Sunday school superintendent and a good church school teacher. Next, he called the artist, Aimee St. Claire forward. She was dressed in a sleeveless linen sheath jade in color with high-heeled pumps dyed to match. Her jet black hair was pulled back in a sophisticated chignon. A single long strand of pearls belonging to her mother with matching earrings completed her elegant ensemble.

Aimee explained why she'd portrayed Christ as smiling and accompanied by children. "Christ loves children for their innocence and spontaneity, their openness and uninhibited joy. As Christ himself said in the Gospel of Luke, Chapter 18, verses 16-18,

But Jesus called for them and said, 'Let the little children come to me, and do not stop them; for it is to such as these that the kingdom of God belongs. Truly I tell you, whoever does not receive the kingdom of God as a little child will never enter it.'

"The figures are life-size and the rainbow signifies the promise of eternal life. The religious mural techniques are ones I learned in Europe. While it is fairly common there, especially in southern France, outdoor murals are rare in this country. Its uniqueness should attract many reverent visitors. I understand that this church will make available a brochure for such visitors with pictures and text so that the Gospel message will be clearly understood." She sat down to a large acclamation of clapping.

Next, the governor was introduced and kept the ceremony short by stating that he couldn't improve on Miss St. Claire's words, but the State of Virginia was very grateful to one of its native artists and wished her well.

Luke pronounced a blessing on the new mural and concluded the ceremony by leading everyone in singing the Doxology. Now, members of the press surged forward to take photographs while firing questions at the governor and Aimee for a little while.

Fairly quickly, the hungry crowd left. A flustered Lydia turned the twins over to their father and went off on Monty's arm.

Chapter Seven

Millie Stewart was in her element as Loch James' "hostess with the moistest." A striped canopy was set up in their backyard to shade the food tables. Two huge standing fans kept air circulating.

"If anyone wants to change and take a dip in the pool while we're setting out lunch, feel free," Millie announced. "My son Dylan, home from the University, has agreed to act as a lifeguard. Wendy, please come with me to help carry trays."

"I'll be glad to help, Mrs. Stewart," Aimee volunteered.

"It's not necessary, Aimee. Why don't you change out of your heels into something more casual? Did you bring a bathing suit?"

"I certainly did," answered Aimee. "But I haven't been swimming for two years. My suit was a Parisian splurge for a last vacation on the French Riviera with my aunt and uncle. The suit may be a bit extreme for a local pool party, so I brought a cover-up."

"I can hardly wait to see it," replied Millie.

"Aimee!" chorused Luke's twins as they arrived for the Stewart's picnic.

"Bonjour," said Aimee. "Our hostess has just suggested a dip in the pool before lunch, so I'm on my way to change into a suit."

"Oh great!" enthused Mandy. "Can I come with you?"

Aimee took her hand and nodded to Luke as they moved off to the assigned changing bedrooms.

"Wow!" said Mandy as she stared at the scanty black, two-piece French bathing suit.

"I want a suit just like yours."

"Your tank suit is appropriate. When you are older and have grown a little more to hold it up, we'll check with your aunt about getting you a two-piece bikini," Aimee replied as she slipped on a black and white cotton cover-up. Then she brushed her hair into a relaxed ponytail, took up her black bathing cap, slipped into her wooden clogs, and draped a beach towel over her shoulder. "Ready?" she asked Mandy.

"Sure thing," Mandy replied and they headed for the pool.

Aimee saw Luke as he and Andy waited by the pool. Luke fairly took Aimee's breath away. There he stood, tall and slim with large shoulders, well-shaped legs—a man fit to be a model for Adonis. He had an arm around Andy's shoulders, and both males smiled broadly as Aimee and Mandy approached.

"The last one in is a slow poke!" Andy challenged his twin. They immediately dropped their towels and dove in like the experienced swimmers they obviously were.

Luke gathered up the kids' towels and turned to Aimee. She was stepping out of her clogs, removed her cover-up and started to tuck her dark hair into her cap. Dylan gave an approving wolf whistle while Luke stood speechless while staring at Aimee's perfectly proportioned curves revealed by her two-piece bathing suit. If he were younger, he might have joined in on Dylan's wolf whistle, but that would not be appropriate for a pastor.

"Ladies first," he said as soon as he could speak.

Aimee snapped her cap, paused gracefully, and then dove in with hardly a splash. Dylan and Luke clapped when Aimee resurfaced.

"What's the clapping about?" Millie demanded as she approached with a tall plastic pitcher of real lemonade.

"Way to go!" shouted Mandy.

"Aimee is a skillful diver," Luke explained and then dove in himself. He was grateful for several years of competitive swimming in college. As he surfaced close to where Aimee was paddling, Luke was careful to keep a comfortable distance since he was so aware of her attractiveness.

Luke called to Dylan. "Come on in!" *There will be safety in number,* he reassured himself. He was acutely aware of her power to arouse his sensuality. *When we go running, we are friendly and enjoy bantering. But this is more serious. It's been a long time…in fact, it's the first time I've reacted to a woman like this since Emily's death. Maybe I'd better play in the shallow water with the twins and leave Dylan and Aimee to their diving.*

Aimee watched Luke move away from her in the pool and how he called his children to join him. An involuntary sense of disappointment overwhelmed her. *He needs to supervise his kids,* she assured herself. *Don't take it personally. Remember his look when he first saw me in my bathing suit! He was all-male at that moment. His eyes smiled approval and I'll remember that.*

Carolyn Crapsey watched from a seat in the shade of an umbrella-topped table. *Darn French flirt!* she said to herself. *Look at her tempting him like that!*

As Millie approached with a cold drink, Carolyn decided to share her anger and indignation. "Aimee's suit is nearly indecent," she commented.

Millie mildly responded with a laugh. "If I had a figure like hers, I'd flaunt it, too."

Carolyn ground her teeth and went in search of other allies in some of the older women spectators on the porch.

"Shocking," agreed one. "I'd never let my daughter appear in a two- piece suit like that in public and certainly not in front of the pastor!"

"I don't know, Caroline. Pastor Luke seems to like her well enough," said another woman.

"Well, she'd never make a proper pastor's wife!" Caroline commented.

At this point, Wendy, Millie Stewart's teen-aged assistant, came out with a tray of appetizers. The ladies on the porch helped themselves and thanked her. As soon as Wendy went back inside, one of the women said, "I feel sorry for poor Wendy—pregnant and abandoned by her family. How charitable of the Stewarts to give her a home."

"Mark my words," Carolyn warned, "they'll live to regret that."

"Debbie is young enough to still need a babysitter, so I think it's a good arrangement, Caroline," countered another elderly church-goer.

"Well, Wendy's not babysitting handsome young Dylan!" Caroline seeded some gossip.

"Yes, he is a handsome young man—the spitting image of his father at that age. Your mother was quite taken with him," reminded another voice.

"Oh yes, well here comes Dylan now carrying a heavy tray for Wendy. Watch them together if you think there's nothing going on there," said Caroline defensively.

The others silently watched the young couple.

"Wendy didn't dare go swimming," Caroline continued. "She's far enough along that she'd be showing in a bathing suit. Does anyone know who the expected baby's father is, by the way?"

"Well, it's NOT Dylan!" thundered a voice from the screen door behind them. Millie stepped out onto her porch as all heads turned toward her. "As her social worker, I KNOW who the father is—a married man if it's any of your business. Dylan and Wendy are friends. Heaven knows Wendy needs all the friends she can get at this point!"

"Of course, Millie," soothed one of the women. "We'll be glad to give her a baby shower when the time comes."

Another turned on Caroline," You should be ashamed of yourself, Caroline! You know how Pastor Luke asked us as Christians to reach out to those less fortunate than ourselves."

"Oh, all right," subsided Caroline. "I'll be glad to help with Wendy's shower, too. Say, isn't it time for lunch?"

"Yes, indeed it is," said Millie. "I was just coming to announce lunch in the big tent."

Everyone was congregating near the big tent. Doc called for quiet, and Luke pronounced grace over the long buffet tables heaped with platters and bowls of fruits, cold meats and, cheeses, salads of every description. It was a potluck feast with separate tables for dessert and drinks. The swimmers had changed into dry, casual attire and the children into shorts and tops. Their suits would hardly be dry before the promised swimming races this afternoon—after the elderly had eaten and gone home for their customary naps.

By 4 p.m. the picnic was winding down. Dylan and Wendy were busy policing up the grounds around the large tent. Doc, as often happened, had been called to the hospital in an emergency.

Luke and his tired twins sought out Millie to say thanks and farewell.

"You two," she said to the twins, "will have to come again and often since you don't have your own pool." They revived enough to assure her they'd be glad to take her up on her offer. Turning to Luke, she said, "I know it was harder for you, Pastor, but I've never seen Lydia as radiant as when she left with Monty. I have something to discuss with you, but it's not urgent, Pastor. I'll call you next week."

When Aimee came up to Millie to thank her for inviting her to the picnic, Millie laughed and hugged her.

"You were the hit of the party, Aimee!" Dylan said as he rounded the corner of the house with a couple of folding chairs. "Paris was obviously good for you."

"If I'd know you would grow up to be so handsome, Dylan, I might have staked a claim," Aimee answered and spontaneously kissed him on both cheeks as the French greet one another.

Wendy, overhearing the remark, hurried to Dylan's side and asked if he would help her with collapsing some folding tables. Millie watched this byplay and began to wonder if Wendy might have a crush on Dylan. Well, it would not hurt her and he could be like a big brother to Wendy.

Aimee thanked Millie once more and got into her truck. She detoured before starting home to take another look at her mural. In the quiet churchyard, she looked up at the face of Christ and suddenly heard the voice of her father: "Daughter, you made me very proud today. But this is just the beginning of your artistic career. With your God-given talent, your works will come to delight thousands."

"Merci, Papa," she replied.

Chapter Eight

The dignitaries had departed, and Monty and Lydia were seated alone on his screened porch waiting for the 9 p.m. fireworks display to begin. "Every year, my wife and I used to come back here for the July 4th fireworks which we funded at Loch James," Monty explained. "Our family has used this lake home since it was built in 1890. My grandfather made a fortune in coal and provided jobs and housing for the mountaineers. What do you think of my home, Lydia?"

"It's breathtaking—such large rooms! Your dining room is one of the largest I've ever seen. Imagine being able to seat twenty guests easily at a single long table! And Monty, your cook is superb. Your daughter Graham is certainly a gracious hostess. 'Graham' is an unusual name."

"It was her mother's maiden name. We waited years for a baby and had nearly given up hope of a child when she finally arrived. That's why she was named Graham…to perpetuate both family names." Lydia nodded her understanding.

"The luncheon party was nicely done, but our private dinner together tonight was even better. I'll never forget it, Lydia," Monty continued. He reached over and took her hand. "Lee, tell me about your life. You've been a widow for fourteen years? How sad."

"Don't say that, Monty. I have been a good mother to Luke's twins and he appreciates me."

"But Lee," Monty protested, "you haven't had much of a life for yourself! Wouldn't' you like to travel and meet more people?"

"Monty, I was never a social butterfly. I like keeping house and caring for our family."

"How about going back to New York City with us?" he asked. "I have a house on Long Island and we can stay there. My plane is right outside of town. Both Graham and I need to get back. Graham's fiancé wants her back in the Big Apple."

"Monty, I'm just a small-town person…not used to jetting around like you," Lydia demurred.

"Well, I think you were still the best looking woman at the parade today. Something tells me you are missing out on life."

Before the conversation could go further, Monty pointed excitedly, "Look, the fireworks are starting! There must be fifty boats out there on the lake. I think we're more comfortable here, though. Usually, I invite many guests to stay and view the fireworks from here, but when I saw you today, I decided to just invite you."

"Why, thank-you, Monty," Lydia said somewhat nervously. "But surely you have many women who'd be glad to spend time with you!"

"I date occasionally. How about you, Lydia? Do you have a significant other?"

"Certainly not. I'm just the widowed aunt who takes care of Luke's home and children. Being with Luke and his twins has given me a real family and a home."

"But what if Luke decides to marry again, Lydia?

"I guess I'd go back to Baltimore. I still have friends there."

"You never thought of remarrying?" he asked.

Blushing, she admitted, "I got a new dress and hairdo for possibly meeting you again."

"Then I came along at the right time," he answered.

"I feel foolish—like a schoolgirl with a crush again."

"We had some good times back in college, didn't we, Lydia? You helped me with my papers and came to all my games. It meant a lot to me that you were in the stands watching. If it hadn't been for that awful war, we might have gotten married!"

"But you went off to Officers Training School and we lost contact. I married my second cousin on the rebound. We were both lonely people and liked a lot of the same things. My mother kind of pushed it, worried I might be an old maid. Garret and I got along well. He was a Navy decoder—a brilliant fellow who loved his books. Only six months after we were married, he was shipped out to Guam. We wrote regularly, but he was one who didn't come home from war. It was hard getting delayed airmail from him after

I knew he'd been killed." She sighed. "That's about it. My memories are short and sweet. "Your turn."

"Well, I was married for a long time to a New York socialite. Our life together consisted of charity balls, going to the theater and the opera, entertaining on a grand scale. I thought when we had a child that she'd settle down. But no! She immediately turned Graham over to a nanny and resumed the high life. I suppose I'd still be part of a whirling social calendar if she hadn't developed cancer and was gone in six months. In some ways, it was a relief to come home to a quiet house and spend time with my daughter. I like to believe I've been a nurturing father to Graham. She couldn't wait to grow up, so she joins my office staff. We are good friends and colleagues as well as father and daughter. I'll certainly miss her when she marries and moves out around this Thanksgiving."

A loud series of bangs and spurting lights appeared over the lake. Cascades of orange and yellow particles lit up the sky and surface of the lake. Bang again. This time it was a fountain of blue and silver streaks. Another pause and a very loud concussion turned into a chrysanthemum. Between aerial displays, there were scenes and figures outlined on giant wooden racks on the long town dock.

Spirited parade music was broadcast in loud volume, and a plane flew overhead—probably carrying photographers. As he watched, Monty thought to himself, *I came back to keep up a family tradition, but have found something different. How can I still be in love with this woman after thirty years without a single contact? It seems crazy, but I know it's true. But will I be able to convince her?*

Lydia sat quietly and also pondered while she watched the fireworks display. *I wonder if it can really be true that after all this time, we might still be meant for each other? God must have sent Monty to me, for I never did anything to precipitate this. If Monty calls tomorrow, I'll know it's not a dream. I'll deal with it then. When I tell Luke, I'll stick to describing this wonderful house and the dinner. He doesn't need to know all those folks left before the fireworks. "I'll bet the twins are excited right now by these fireworks!"* she said aloud.

After the spectacular finish with the red, white, and blue United States flag burning the night sky and rockets flying in all directions, the music fell silent, and boat motors started up noisily.

"I'd better get home now to help Luke get the children off to bed. This has been a wonderful day, Monty. I'm coming to love life among these Blue Ridge Mountains."

"July is a beautiful time of the year but wait until you see our spectacular fall colors!" Monty said. "I always come again in October, and you can be sure I'll come this year with you here, Lydia."

He summoned the limousine to transport them to the parsonage. On the way, he asked if Luke was enjoying being pastor of the Community Church.

"It's his dream come true—a rural church where he can really get to know his people and make a difference in their lives."

"I noticed," probed Monty, "that Pastor Luke has eyes for the pretty French artist Aimee St. Claire. Do you think the attraction is mutual?'

"You'll have to ask Luke. I know both of the twins love her."

"I knew Aimee's father. He painted that picture of our summer home you saw in the library—with Graham playing in the sand and a rainbow overhead. He made a fair living with his landscapes and was a terrific teacher who encouraged art among young people. I remember he said he was drawn to these mountains and didn't ever go home to France. Incidentally, he married a beautiful local girl; that's where Aimee got her looks."

Realizing that they were nearly back to the parsonage, Monty asked, "Could I see you sometime tomorrow morning, Lydia, before we leave? If you can't go with us to New York this time, perhaps we can arrange a more convenient time with a couple of weeks' advance warning. I think you'd love to go to some Broadway stage plays, visit museums and art galleries, and see beautiful Long Island Sound where we live. I know I'll come down here for a week next month and we can get better reacquainted. Now that I've found you again, I don't want to lose you."

"Monty, what a romantic you are! I'm a trifle old to be swept off my feet, though. Not that I won't be glad to see you when you come back," she hastily added.

The limo slowed to a stop in the parsonage driveway. "Why don't you come for coffee tomorrow about ten--after the twins are off to the playground and tennis lessons?"

Monty walked Lydia to the porch. As she turned to say good-night, Monty took her into his arms and kissed her. Lydia's heart pounded and she began to respond when Luke suddenly put on the porch light and they sprang apart like guilty teenagers.

"Sorry!" said Luke and laughed from embarrassment and surprise.

Monty recovered composure first. "I'm just returning Lydia after a lovely evening," he explained. "How did you folks like the fireworks?"

"They were really spectacular for such a small town," was Luke's opinion.

"Someone told me we owe them all to you. My twins were very impressed, too. They babbled all the way home."

Lydia spoke up. "Thanks again, Monty. 'See you in the morning for coffee."

"You bet, Lydia," he replied, quickly hugged her and went back to the waiting limo. The driver sprang out, opened the rear door for Monty, and then took his place behind the wheel. Immediately the long car pulled away out of the drive.

"Well, well, well, Mrs. Hammond," Luke began.

"Not now, Luke. I'm too tired. Today was wonderful but almost too much for your old aunt."

"You're not my OLD aunt, Lydia, but a very attractive lady obviously," Luke replied.

"Thank you, Luke. Good night." She was humming to herself as she climbed the stairs.

Lydia dressed more carefully than usual the next morning in white slacks and a sleeveless blue top with her best white sandals. Instead of just brushing her hair and dabbing on a bit of lipstick, Lydia took time for full makeup while the coffee perked. Then she set the kitchen table for the children's and Luke's healthy breakfasts of fruit, orange juice, plus a variety of cold cereals.

This is a far cry from that huge dining room table at Monty's last night with linen tablecloths and napkins," she thought. *I certainly feel more comfortable here.*

Luke came in hurriedly, having overslept. "I'll just grab a cup of coffee," he stipulated. "I have a nine o'clock appointment at the church office. Say, you're looking pretty spiffy this morning. What time is Monty coming?"

"He's just coming for coffee ahead of leaving town," Lydia said defensively.

"He's leaving already?"

"His Lear jet is whisking him and his daughter Graham back to New York City," Lydia explained. "In fact, he asked me to go with them."

"Great, Lydia. I'll find someone to watch the children while you're gone," he said, surprising her.

"Luke, I can't just go flying off without leaving meals ready and being sure the children have supervision," Lydia protested.

"Why not, Lydia? You've certainly earned a vacation after eleven years. I'll see to the needs of my family. Call me if you decide to go," and Luke hurried off.

"Who's coming to breakfast, Aunt Lydia?" asked Mandy, who had overheard the previous adults' conversation. "Do I need to get dressed before I eat?"

"Please do, Mandy, and shake Andy if he's not already up," Lydia ordered. She poured herself a cup of coffee while she waited.

"Okay, I'm dressed," Mandy stated the obvious a few minutes later. "Who's coming to breakfast…Mr. Montgomery?"

"You've big ears, Miss Mandy. For your information, I'm entertaining someone for coffee long after you and your brother have left for the summer program at the schoolyard."

Andy clumped down the stairs next and began peeling himself a banana. "Can I have Wheaties today?"

Mandy scoffed. "I suppose you want to be a champion again at soccer practice…like two days ago when you tripped over the ball and fell flat!"

"Now, Mandy," interceded Lydia. "Not everyone is as well coordinated as you are. As long as your brother enjoys his soccer like you enjoy your tennis, he's doing fine."

There was a knock at the front door. Monty stood there. "I couldn't wait any longer to see you, Lee. May I come in?"

As she opened the door, Mandy piped up. "Lee? How come you call Aunt Lydia 'Lee'?"

"Are you Amanda all the time?" he asked.

"No, I'm Mandy most of the time 'cept when I do something wrong. Then I'm 'Amanda Grace.' Oh, you meant that Lee is Aunt Lydia's nickname?"

"No," he said, "it is a favorite name I called my girlfriend over thirty-five years ago."

"Please"…Lydia interrupted, "let's not get into how long ago that was."

"You're still a beauty, Lee," Monty said and kissed her on the cheek.

"Wow," said Andy, his eyes wide. "Wait until I tell Dad!"

"Never mind, I'll tell your father," Lydia said. "Now, fold your napkins and say a polite good-morning to Mr.

Montgomery. If you don't get along right away, you'll be late for your lessons at the playground."

The twins did as they were told and went off down the street on their bikes trying to take the lead. "I win," floated back, but Lydia wasn't sure which twin's voice it was. There was a sudden quiet after the screen door had slammed behind the twins.

"Cute kids," commented Monty. "How about giving me a real kiss, Lee? I've waited so long."

"Well, one kiss… but we really need to talk, Monty. Then I'll get us some coffee. Monty stood up and held out his arms. Lydia went eagerly into them and her arms lifted to go around his neck. Their lips met softly for a slight time. Then Lydia pulled away. "It HAS been a very long time, Monty."

They sat across from one another over second cups of coffee. She said, "Yesterday was absolutely wonderful, Monty. The supper and fireworks were especially lovely. I could hardly sleep for thinking about you and reviewing the details of the day. But, as you can see, it's back to normalcy."

"I like the warmth of your cheery kitchen, Lee, and your interactions with your niece and nephew. I often find myself very lonely."

"What if I did not go away with you, but you came here, Monty? Then we could truly get reacquainted." She shook her head. "It's just very hard for me to believe you're seriously interested in me."

"Okay, I'll fly back for weekends, and I've already planned on two weeks here in October for the fall colors."

"You'd fly back from New York every weekend to see me?" Lydia marveled.

"Well, Friday afternoon at corporate headquarters is not usually too busy, and I can arrange not to have meetings until Monday afternoon," Monty explained.

Lydia looked at this distinguished man, dressed in expensive casual slacks and a sports shirt with loafers. Sunglasses peeked out of his shirt pocket. He still moved with much vigor and looked happier than yesterday when all dressed up as a dignitary. His blue eyes were sparkling and his face was tanned, his small mustache gray-peppered as was his dark hair. That hair was still abundant and he'd kept himself trim and fit. He certainly didn't look his age.

"Won't your daughter miss you if you come here so often?"

"Oh, I'm quite superfluous right now. Her friends and fiancé keep her occupied, and she's planning a September wedding for which I'll be footing the bills. However, since Graham's my only child, I don't mind. Graham and her fiancé will be welcome to come down here with me. Her childhood included many happy occasions in Loch James. I used to tease her about going to the coal mines and fixing them up, but she has become my capable assistant and will take over Montgomery Coal and Mining Corporation with holdings all over the world when I retire. She met Bret Cabot in Argentina when they were both attending to family interests there."

"Do you like him?" Lydia asked.

"Oh yes. He's the son I always wanted. They're a handsome couple and should give me beautiful grandchildren. And speaking of Graham, she's probably pacing the plane right now, so I'd better be on my way. How about my calling you this evening, OK?"

"Why, yes," agreed the overwhelmed Lydia. She was having difficulty keeping up with the pace of this relationship.

At the door, she quickly kissed him on both cheeks lightly. "Bon voyage, you industry captain," she told him. "I'll look forward to seeing you on Friday, Monty."

"Until tonight, Love," he responded and hurried off to the car to be on his way to the waiting plane.

Lydia was still rocking herself in the porch swing when she heard the roar of the Lear Jet leaving. "Lord," she whispered, "when You get around to sending gifts to Your faithful servants, You really are generous! Thank-you. Amen."

Chapter Nine

Luke's part-time secretary, Miss Cora McPherson, stopped her word-processing of notes to sick parishioners. "Good morning, Pastor Luke. You are prompt this morning after the big holiday."

"Miss Cora, it's a gorgeous morning, the mural is done and dedicated, and the good life in Loch James goes on."

Just then, Millie Stewart came rushing in. Pastor Luke welcomed her and instructed Cora to hold all calls except for emergencies. Then he invited Millie into his study. She was wearing matching shorts set and sandals.

"Won't you sit down, Millie?"

"No, I'd rather stand. I'm so peeved at how some of the older so-called ladies are treating Wendy. She's pregnant all right, but hardly showing yet. Already the women are whispering maliciously about who the father of Wendy's baby is."

Luke gulped. "I didn't even know Wendy is pregnant. I just thought she was a friend of your family who is helping out this summer in return for room and board."

"Well, you're new here, Pastor Luke. Wendy's family disowned her as soon as they learned she was pregnant, so Doc and I invited her to stay with us for the duration. The actual father is a married man. I'm not going to tell you who, but he doesn't go to this church. So poor Wendy is facing this pregnancy alone."

She continued. "The only reason I know about the father is that Wendy specified he not be contacted about anything concerning herself or the baby."

"So the real father doesn't know she is pregnant?"

"Probably not. Her folks feel disgusted and disgraced, so they've thrown her out."

"Poor child," said Luke.

"She's eighteen, so they don't have to keep her. When she went to Doc for medical advice, she was adamant about wanting to keep her baby. Doc discussed it with me, and we agreed that our home is large enough to provide her shelter during the waiting and beyond—until she can become independent."

"You don't think it might do any good for me to visit her family?" Luke asked.

"They're fundamentalists and believe she is paying the price for her sinning," Millie explained. "I'd hoped we of the Community Church would prove ourselves more compassionate," she added.

"And so we shall," Luke agreed. "This church family will become Wendy's loving family. In fact, my sermon this Sunday will concern Christ's warning to some hypocritical men about to stone a woman to death when they themselves are living less than perfect lives."

"Wendy's a nice girl," Millie went on. "She got into trouble because she didn't have love at home and was searching for it in the wrong places. In order for her to become a loving parent, she needs to experience a loving environment in which her self-respect is reinforced. Luke, I don't want to get you in trouble with the older women, but I just have to fight for Wendy."

"That's very commendable of you and Doc. Do you think Wendy might become a member of the junior choir and youth group here at the church?"

"I'll ask her. She's pretty lonely right now, so I think she'll agree. Aside from studying for her high school equivalency test, she mostly reads and watches television when she's not helping me. She needs young friends desperately."

"How about Aimee?" asked Luke. "She's pretty broad minded after her time in France."

"Great idea, Pastor. Aimee's so vivacious and young enough to not talk down to Wendy. In fact, she's great with young people generally."

"I've been thinking along the same lines," Luke agreed. "Aimee would make a great Adult Youth Volunteer if she'd take the job. Her music would be a real plus with young people."

"Well, I've got to run along," Millie said. "You can be sure I'll be listening to your special sermon on Sunday."

There was a jingle of bells and the sound of hooves on the cobblestones outside. Luke was just escorting Millie to the door.

Cora looked out of the side window. "Speak of an angel and there she appears—Miss Aimee herself. I wonder why she's here now when her mural's all finished."

"Good," said Millie. "Luke, why don't you ask her about helping with the Youth Group?"

Luke responded, "I shall as soon as we have appropriate time. She's not a regular attendee, you know."

Cora inserted, "But her father and mother were faithful members."

Luke disliked being pushed to do something precipitously. "All in good time, ladies," he assured them. He also wondered why Aimee had come…since they hadn't jogged together this morning. He watched her for a few minutes while she set up a tripod and began to take a series of pictures of her mural. He rather doubted that photography would bring her into the church office.

"I'll be back shortly," he told Cora and went out to offer his help. It was a flimsy excuse, he conceded to himself. Aimee looked attractive in clean jeans, a Western shirt, and well-worn cowboy boots as she strode about taking pictures from various angles.

"How about I take a picture of you beside the mural?" he suggested.

"Oh, I'm not dressed for a picture," she refused. "You could steady a ladder for me so I can snap a close-up of the face of Christ."

"Sure," he agreed. *Any excuse to spend time with Aimee,* he admitted to himself. "Shall we go jogging tomorrow?" he asked.

"Well, I'll be going anyway, so you're welcome to join me," she said.

"It's getting warm enough that it'd be good to go for a dip afterward in a pool," he said to continue the discussion.

"I have my own swimming hole," she said. "When I'm home next weekend, how about you and the children coming up for a swim?"

"It sounds wonderful," he agreed. "I'll call before we come." He helped her load up her photographic equipment, waved her off, and went whistling back to his study. Eluding Cora, who unsuccessfully tried to worm out of Luke the purpose for Millie's visit, he began work on the promised sermon.

As Luke sauntered home for lunch, he mentally reviewed again the main points for Sunday's sermon. He was troubled and the sermon was not coming easily. *Maybe I can run this crisis about Wendy by Lydia. She's always been a good sounding board for me.*

Lydia dished up some homemade vegetable soup and cornbread for the twins' and Luke's lunch. They added syrup to their cornbread, ate quickly, and washed it all down with large glasses of milk. Mandy reported she was improving her soccer game under a teenage coach.

Andy pooh-poohed her achievements "'cause she's on a girls' team and they don't play nearly as rough as our boys' teams do."

Rough or not, they were both eager to return to the playground for their afternoon games. Lydia made sure each twin had enough spending money for a popsicle on the way home at Mort Culpepper's Drugstore.

"Be sure to introduce yourselves to Mr. Culpepper and tell him I send him my greetings," Luke ordered them. They hastily agreed, took one last chocolate chip cookie apiece for the road, and then left—letting the screen door bang behind them.

"How about some hot coffee, Luke? asked Lydia in the new quiet.

"Thanks," said Luke. "Could I run something by you, Lydia? It concerns some women at the church and is confidential."

"My lips are sealed, Luke. What's going on?" asked Lydia.

"Millie Stewart came to see me this morning. It seems some of our older ladies are chit-chattering about young Wendy and speculating about who her unborn baby's father is."

"Wendy is pregnant?" asked a surprised Lydia.

"Yes, and the Stewarts have decided to befriend her by letting her stay with them during her pregnancy and until she can provide for the baby and herself. Her folks have disowned her."

"How charitable of the Stewarts!" commented Lydia.

"Well, I intend to challenge my flock with my sermon next Sunday—exhorting them to be careful about casting stones at others when they are leading less than perfect lives themselves—that we need to deal compassionately with one another because all of us need God's compassion and forgiveness."

"Be careful, Luke. You are new here and it's too soon for your people to know and trust you well. Maybe you can go about this in a quieter way."

"Like what, Lydia?"

"Well, if it were up to me, I'd probably call on a couple of the women leaders—like Ruth Johnson, who's President of the Ladies Missionary Society and Natalie Sherwood, the Superintendent of the Sunday school. They're very influential, so if you get their support, they can swing the other women around."

"Thanks, Lydia! I'll see each of them personally tomorrow. Remind me to wear my clerical collar."

"You do look more impressive in your collar, Luke."

"If this works, I can be more general in my sermon. Actually, I don't believe in scolding a whole class for the misdeeds of a few. You're a genius, Lydia!"

"No, Luke, just a woman who understands how the Lord often works in quiet and mysterious ways."

Luke left to return to the church. He was humming and thinking about jogging with Aimee tomorrow morning.

Luke woke before the alarm clock could sound off at six. He slipped into his jogging outfit, thick socks, and new running shoes. He stopped for a glass of juice and then headed for the rendezvous point at the trailhead.

Why am I so eager this morning—just to be doing something with Aimee or to ask her to be a friend to Wendy as Millie suggests? We're really only friends since Aimee is not attending my church regularly, but I hope she will agree to befriend Wendy. That could be a first step toward getting Aimee involved with our church family.

Luke pulled into a parking place and noted Aimee's truck approaching. She pulled in alongside of him and jumped out.

"Good morning, Luke. Are you ready? Let's stretch first."

They put their feet against something solid, bent over to stretch their muscles, shook their arms to loosen up, and started at a slow jog in the beginning.

"Beautiful morning," commented Luke after ten minutes when they'd slowed to a fast walk. Aimee was getting him prepared gradually for longer distances by alternating jogging and fast walking.

"Yes, it is," she agreed.

"Millie Stewart came to see me yesterday," he began again.

"Oh? Why?"

"She's concerned about Wendy's being pregnant and talked about."

"Wendy's pregnant?" Aimee asked. "I just thought she was a friend of Dylan's."

"No, Wendy's family has disowned her and the Stewarts took her in."

"Mon Dieu! She's too young to be on her own, especially while pregnant! She certainly needs to finish high school."

"Millie has her studying already for her high school equivalency exam, but Millie feels that Wendy needs some friends, especially since some of the older women are being catty about her condition."

"That's terrible!"

"Well, I've written a sermon reminding people how unchristian finding fault with others is, but Lydia had a good idea about a more direct approach."

"Oh?"

"She suggested I call on some opinion leaders among the women to offset the gossip."

"Good idea!" approved Aimee.

"That still doesn't speak to Wendy's loneliness, however."

Aimee immediately caught his drift. "Are you suggesting I become her friend, Luke?"

"Well, give it some thought, will you? I think you could be a very good influence on her. Most of her classmates and her own family have abandoned her, but you are young enough to hear her sympathetically and not judge her."

They picked up their pace again and nothing was said for the next ten minutes.

As they slowed again, Aimee spoke. "Okay, Luke. I'll talk to Wendy and we'll see where it goes from there. Maybe she would like to be my assistant in Roanoke. That'd take her out of town for a while and we'd get to know one another better. I'll make the offer anyway. Should I approach Millie with the idea first?"

"That might be best since the Stewarts have made themselves responsible for her. Meanwhile, I'll call on the women's leaders to defuse the gossip." That agreed, they went into another jogging phase. As they once again slowed, Luke asked, "Where will you be staying while in Roanoke?"

"The Baptists have just purchased a piece of adjoining land with a small cottage on it which they'll eventually use to house an assistant minister. They've agreed to let me stay there this summer, and there'll be lots of room for Wendy if she wants to come along. In fact, I'd appreciate the company."

"Thank you, Aimee. This is my first pastoral crisis and you've helped me deal with it. Let me know what Millie thinks of the scheme. How soon do you start at Roanoke?"

"I allowed myself a few days of rest, but I'll be going over this Thursday and Friday to make arrangements, submit sketches for final approval, and purchase materials."

"So soon?" said Luke involuntarily.

"I'll be back late Friday night, Luke. We can jog on Saturday," she answered. The fact that he would miss her pleased Aimee, but she noted from his high color that he'd embarrassed himself by expressing how much he would miss her.

By the time they arrived back at their vehicles, Luke was winded and Aimee breathing heavily. They both drank thirstily from the spring-fed fountain and then walked about to cool down.

Luke consulted his watch. He'd been gone an hour and needed to get home in time for a shower and breakfast with his family.

Aimee wiped her face and arms with a large towel. Then she said in a teasing voice, "You'll need to use even more of your persuasive charm on the OLDER ladies, Luke. Lean on the fact that you NEED their help…and you do! Shall we meet again tomorrow and you can tell me how you did?"

"Pray for me, Aimee. I'll need all the help I can get."

"On praying, I'm a bit rusty, but for you, I'll try," and she climbed into her truck and headed back up the mountain.

Along the jogging trail the next day, Aimee queried Luke about visiting the two older women.

"Aimee, I shortchanged a couple of good women. Lucille Heatherton broke down and cried when I explained how hurt Millie was by the gossip about Wendy. She'll do everything in her power to make amends. Janice Whitcomb was a bit harder nut, but she's coming around, too. Neither woman meant to be cruel. It's just how anything new balloons in sleepy, small towns. Janice will help organize a baby shower for Wendy."

"That's great, Luke. I knew you could do it," Aimee congratulated him. "Besides, I even prayed and how could God resist that? Remember, it's God who gets the real credit for the turnaround."

"Of course, Aimee, and I'm happy you realize that."

"By the way, Wendy is going to be traveling back and forth to Roanoke with me. Lizzie really likes the idea I'll not be alone and Millie approves. Besides, Wendy can earn a few dollars and still have time to study."

"You can't afford to pay her, Aimee. Let me subsidize her wages from my discretionary fund," Luke offered.

"If you insist," Aimee agreed, "but just enough she has some spending money. I'll pay her and let you know how much if you want to reimburse me."

They speeded up, but at the next walking interval, Luke brought up the subject of Lydia and Monty's romance. "Have you noticed how Lydia has bloomed since Monty began calling every night and returning on weekends?"

"He calls her every night?" Aimee checked.

"Yes, and sends her flowers every other day or so," Luke added. "He asked when her birthday will be, and it sounds like he's planning to give her a Mercedes two-seater."

"My goodness! It sounds serious," Aimee commented. "Lydia has always been a pleasant, neat person, but now… she just glows. I think she's in love! Luke, what will you and the children do if she decides to marry Monty?"

"We'll be all right. Lydia deserves her happiness. I'll just have to make other arrangements," Luke said bravely. "The kids are getting older and more responsible. With God's help, we'll manage."

Chapter Ten

"Please be seated," Luke invited the congregation after the Gospel, Luke 13:1-9, had been read. In the front row, Lydia waited expectantly for the special sermon Luke had indicated he would be preaching this morning. It would speak obliquely to Wendy's plight as an unwed mother and people's attitudes toward her. "After all," as Luke had told her, "Our Lord used parables to make His points."

Luke began by pointing out that in this rural community, many could appreciate that a barren tree should be destroyed and replaced by one that would bear fruit:

The fruits in a Christian's life include caring, loving, good works, charity, and common sense. The owner in the story rushes to judgment and orders the barren fig tree to be uprooted and destroyed. The vintner, however, in Christ's role as intercessor, pleads for another chance. He will help the poor tree by cultivating the soil around its roots and adding fertilizer.

With practice and caring helpfulness, the fig tree is able to produce flowers and fruit. The owner, as God is portrayed in this parable, is pleased with both the tree and the one who assisted it to fulfill its destiny.

"So..." Luke concludes as he carefully sweeps the whole congregation with his eyes, "let us be careful about rushing to judgment and diligent about helping those less fortunate than ourselves. We are bidden to love others as much as God loves each of us. Remember in The Lord's Prayer, we will be forgiven our trespasses in exact proportion to how "we forgive those who trespass against us."

A potent silence followed Pastor Luke as he sat down for the customary quiet time following each sermon. Luke noticed several women who had tears on their faces, so he knew that the message had been received. *Thank you, Holy Spirit,* Luke prayed, then rose again to lead another hymn.

After the benediction, quite a few parishioners shook Luke's hand and remarked on the sermon. Millie congratulated and thanked him in particular. Aimee leaned over to whisper, "You really got them, Rev! 'Good going!" Then she straightened and said loudly, "We'll be expecting you and the children up on the mountain as soon as you can make it. Don't forget your bathing suits."

An hour later, Luke and the children were driving up the mountain road toward Painter's Pond. Mandy kept pointing out squirrels and birds. Then they came to the pasture where the thoroughbred horses looked up from their gazing.

Clem greeted them in the circular drive. Andy immediately asked if they could ride the horses.

"Not today, Andy. Lizzie has packed a picnic for you folks to hike on up to the waterfall."

"Cool," responded Mandy.

"That it is," said Clem. That waterfall is fed by streams from mountain springs and the water is cold except in a few shallow places where the sun warms it."

"I already have my bathing suit on under my clothes," Mandy explained.

Aimee emerged onto the porch. "Where are my pack animals for this lunch so we can get started up the mountain?"

"I'll be a pack animal," Mandy volunteered. "I can carry this big thermos jug."

Not to be outdone, Andy tried picking up the big basket. Luke said, "You'd better let me help you with that, son." They could tote it walking side by side.

"How far is it from here?" Luke asked.

"Only five minutes from here. You can hear the waterfall on quiet nights—like a big fountain," Aimee assured them. She carried a stack of towels and her sketching satchel. Soon she led the way up a steep path where rocks were placed for firm footing. The gushing sounds grew gradually louder and there was moss on the rocks. One last turn and they stood looking up at a small, but high waterfall. The sunlight glinted off the rushing waters.

To their right were some steps which Clem had chipped into the rocks so one could go behind the falling water into a cave. "Can we go back there?" asked Mandy.

"Let's eat our lunch first before we explore," ordered Luke. "And don't go back there without an adult with you!" he added.

Aimee spread a blanket and they each sat on one corner while she unpacked Lizzie's fried chicken, potato salad, potato chips, celery and carrot sticks, homemade rolls, with sponge cake and peaches for dessert washed down with pink lemonade. Luke said grace and they filled their plastic plates and ate with plastic forks. Lots of paper napkins helped with sticky fingers.

Mandy looked at her large drumstick. "This isn't from one of your geese, is it?" she asked.

"Certainly not!" laughed Aimee. "Those geese are members of our family like your puppies are of yours." The supply of food was drastically reduced in the next few minutes.

Andy finished first and asked to be excused. His father said, "Wait a minute. Aren't you going to wait for dessert?"

"Aw, Dad, I want to go and see what's up the path."

"Wait for your sister and the rest of us to finish eating," Luke instructed Andy.

Andy resumed his seat reluctantly and turned to Aimee. "Did you know my dad is a Good Samaritan? He gave a hitchhiker a ride."

"Did he now?" asked Aimee with a good deal of interest. "I'm not allowed to pick up hitchhikers—too dangerous."

Luke felt obliged to explain. "We merely assisted a stranded motorist."

Mandy spoke up, "The man gave us some good apples for helping him, and he said Dad was a Good Samaritan."

Luke broke in quickly. "I write children's stories for a Sunday School publisher."

Aimee said, "Tell me exactly what your father said and did. She took up her sketch pad and quickly animated what they were telling her in a series of sketches. There was the man standing in the road, and then Luke's handing him a cellular phone. The next sketch showed them riding together in Luke's car, and finally—the man presenting some apples to Luke.

"He even told us his mother used to go to Dad's church!" Mandy added.

"Those are neat sketches!" admired Andy.

"Let me see," requested Luke. "My word, you've captured the likeness so well with just a few lines. I don't suppose I could talk you into becoming my illustrator on a regular basis? Your drawings would more than double the value of my stories to my publisher.

"Yes. I'll push you to tell the stories more often if we're being paid," Aimee assured him.

Mandy said, "You know, Dad, Aimee painted your picture on the mural and when I spoke to her about it, she changed it!"

"Is that true, Aimee?" asked Luke.

"Well, it wasn't intentional, Luke...that I saw your face as something like Christ's."

Aimee was blushing as she turned to the twins. "How about you two picking some asters for Lizzie—to thank her for such a nice lunch? There should be some in that meadow off to the right. Just follow the path, but don't go into the woods. You might want to scatter some petals along the path to see it better on your way back. By the time you do that, it'll be time to go for a swim." The twins sprang up, intrigued by their assignment, and went off in the direction indicated.

"Aimee, did you really paint my likeness in that mural?"

"Well, there was something about Christ's smile that made Mandy think of you, so I changed it in case any of your parishioners thought the same thing."

"Actually, I'm complimented, Aimee, but I'm glad you didn't leave it that way. Speaking of murals, how is Wendy working out as your assistant?"

"She's a fine girl and I enjoy her company. Definitely, she's a good worker and is gaining some self-confidence. I've promised her a good work reference and she should pass her GED test without difficulty so she'll have the equivalent of a high school certificate."

"Did you know that Wendy has a strong, true alto singing voice? When we're traveling, we often harmonize on hymns, fold music, and country-western songs. She's taught me some of the newer country-western songs!"

"That's great, Aimee. You're really good with young people. Between that and your musical ability, I've been seriously considering asking you to become one of our Youth Leaders this coming year."

"Luke, that's a big jump for someone who only attends church once in a while. Let me think it over, OK? Say, doesn't that mean I'd be taking on the annual mountainside Christmas pageant?"

"I guess, but I've not been here at Christmas. Tell me about the Christmas pageant," Luke requested.

"If I remember rightly," Aimee explained, "almost everybody gets involved. My father furnished the sheep for the illuminated manger scene halfway up to the mountain. He sent Clem along as a shepherd to help keep order among the four-footed actors.

"Then there's Phil MacDougall, the electrician, who has enough lights on that permanent stage to light up every street in Loch James. His son, young Phil, manages the sound system every year. But the human actors change every year—chosen by the Youth Group. The townspeople gather down below to sing carols, alternating with the young people far up the mountain beyond the manger scene. Of course, the baby is the youngest citizen of Loch James, whether a boy or a girl.

"People come from quite a distance to see this pageant and the merchants do very well, so they fund the expenses, especially when Elder Crapsey goes around collecting. We celebrate afterward at the church with wassail, hot chocolate, and Christmas cookies. Any profits go into Christmas baskets for the poor around the county."

Luke pondered all this and said, "Strange that the Calling Committee didn't mention this project to me."

"It sounds just overwhelming," said Aimee.

"Let me assure you that the entire congregation will help you with this traditional event, Aimee. You'd mainly be in charge of the young people's part of the music."

"I'll think it over," Aimee said again.

Luke decided to not press her any harder, especially since the twins were returning with their bouquets of wildflowers, and he didn't want them involved in this matter. Aimee quickly filled the wide-mouthed thermos with water and consolidated their bouquets to take back to Lizzie.

"Time to go swimming yet?" Mandy asked.

"Yes. You may want to stay in the shallower water along the edge of the pool where the sun has warmed the water," Aimee advised them.

"Are you going to go in, Daddy?" challenged Andy.

"Sure am, son." Luke was peeling off his tee-shirt and trousers to reveal his swimming trunks.

Aimee was wearing a wrap-around skirt, and when she stepped out of her sandals, skirt, and blouse, she was ready to swim in a sedate white, one-piece bathing suit. Mandy, watching Aimee, approved the single-piece suit much like her own.

"The last one in is a toad!" shouted Mandy heading for the water. She stopped suddenly at knee-depth, her arms crossed over her chest. "Wow, this is cold!" she lamented.

Andy entered the water more gingerly. "C'mon, Aimee. It's not that bad. I'm waiting for you!" he encouraged her.

"Well, I don't want to be a toad," she laughed and splashed water on her arms and shoulders to help get used to the cool water.

"Oh, well…" said Luke. "I may be the toad, but maybe a pretty girl will kiss me and turn me into a prince."

Aimee loved his reference to the old French fairy tale. "Mon Dieu, I'll save you," and she splashed over and kissed him playfully on both cheeks. How Luke wished suddenly they were alone together, but now everyone was laughing and splashing, having a high old time.

Andy was the first to get out and wrap himself in a towel. "Let's go see the cave now," he suggested. The others were ready for an activity change, so they went exploring in their bathing suits.

"This way," led Aimee up the steps beside the waterfall and then quickly jumped to the floor of the cave just above the rushing waters.

"It's kind of dark back in here," quavered Andy.

"Look back that way," directed Aimee, "and you'll see daylight at the back entrance. One of the best things about this cave is that it's an echo chamber."

"An echo chamber? What's that?" demanded Mandy.

"If you stand right back here on this slab of rock where Clem marked the spot, you can throw your voice and hear an echo out over the waterfall and down the mountain," she explained. "Let me show you." Aimee pushed her voice from her diaphragm and projected a protracted "Hello!"

There was a hush and then a softer "Hello" echoed back.

"Oh, how neat! Let me try it," volunteered Mandy.

"Climb up here beside me," instructed Aimee. "Now, what are you going to say?"

"How about I say 'Good-bye'?"

"Okay, try it," Aimee said.

"GOOD-BYE!" shouted Mandy

"Good-bye" floated back tersely.

"You must speak slowly and give the echo time to resonate," coached Aimee.

"Sometimes I sing a line at a time and then wait for it to echo before I sing another line."

"Oh, I bet that sounds pretty!" admired Mandy.

"Let's sing something. Do you know 'Frere Jacques'?" Aimee asked.

"Sure, Daddy taught us. He speaks French very well," Mandy replied.

Ah, another thing we have in common! Aimee thought. *How like Luke to just let me discover this. Oh dear, then he knew what I was saying when I said 'Mon Dieu.' Well, too late now.*

"This should be interesting," Luke agreed. "Does the mountain echo pick up more than one singing part?"

"Whatever is projected from here," Aimee replied. "Crowd together on the ledge now. Are we all ready? Remember, let the echo be the repetition for each line. Observe a slight pause and then begin the next line. Watch me, and I'll cue us so we stay together."

"Frere Jacques…" they sang and the mountain echo obediently repeated their singing.

"Dormez-Vous"…etc. The little old French refrain echoed down the mountain. The children were entranced, and far below Lizzie and Clem smiled at one another. When the song faded, Lizzie said, "I think our Aimee has found a new family."

Soon, the picnickers returned and Luke loaded the twins up. Then he thanked Aimee, Lizzie, and Clem for their hospitality and headed back to the parsonage with his tired but happy twins.

Aimee sat watching the sunset later on the porch swing while enjoying the evening sounds—soft cooing of doves and the singing of tree toads. As she identified the sound of the tree toads, she thought of the verbal exchange with Luke this afternoon that led on to his request regarding helping the Youth Group.

Am I considering taking the job to see more of Luke or because I may be a good influence on some young lives? Certainly, it will mean using my musical training. Now, who am I kidding? Sure, my motives are mixed, but I honestly know I enjoy being with Luke and his children. What fun we had today! How his children love him! When he's alone with them, he's actually playful.

Maybe I should pray about it before giving him an answer as he suggested. I don't want leading the Youth Group to be a selfish thing. I know. I'll run it by Lizzie. She's religious and she certainly knows me.

—m—

The following Saturday, Aimee was waiting in her truck at the trailhead for Luke to appear for jogging. She was rehearsing how to tell Luke that despite reservations, she was going to accept his challenge to help lead the Youth Group. She'd do so on a six-month trial basis. Lizzie had suggested the trial period to overcome Aimee's self-doubts.

I'm certainly enjoying Wendy's company. Since Wendy will be the oldest member of the Youth Group, I'll depend on her as lead alto singer. Yeah, this should work! Oops, here comes Luke.

"You beat me today. Do I get an answer today about the Youth Group? I don't mean to hurry you, but I need to know."

"I will take it on a six-month basis, Luke. If you or I decide at the end of that time that it is not working out, then you'll find someone else to help."

Luke breathed a sigh of relief. Six months would take them past the Christmas Pageant. He reached over and lovingly hugged her. "Bless you, Aimee. I'm confident that this will be one of the best years ever for our Youth Group."

As they jogged along side by side, Aimee spoke up. "One good turn deserves another, don't you think?"

Cautiously Luke agreed. "So what are you asking, Aimee?" he asked with a grin.

"If you and the twins can make it, I'd like you to attend the dedication of my Roanoke mural at the Baptist Church on Saturday afternoon, Sept. 28th."

"I don't have my calendar in my shorts pocket, but that should be all right. I'll try to have all the office work and my sermon done by Friday so I can—aside from the actual church services—spend the weekend with the twins. Actually, I'm curious to see what you've been working on there. This mural is one of the Good Samaritan, didn't you tell me?"

"Come and see," she teased him gently. The Baptists are hosting a barbeque afterward. Their Youth Group is singing for the occasion. Hey, maybe we should take our entire Youth Group."

"There's nothing the youth like better than an outing. You're already thinking like their leader," he assured her.

"I'll check with the Baptist Pastor, but I'm sure he'd be glad to add a dozen young people to the crowd," Aimee enthused. "Maybe he could be persuaded to have our Junior Choir on the program for a musical number...a deadline to help rally our youth from the beginning of September."

"That's a good idea, Aimee! I'll announce the first meeting of the Youth Group for the Sunday evening after Labor Day, but you can tell them about the music and the outing. Speaking of September, I'm wondering about Wendy's traveling so much with you now that she's into her last trimester."

"She's already told me that she'll not be going with me in September...too close to her due date in early November, although I'm sure she'll want to come to the dedication."

"I guess that will be up to Dr. Stewart. Perhaps Millie and he could drive her in the car for a smoother ride than the rented school bus," suggested Luke.

"Great idea, Luke! We're getting to be quite a team!"

Chapter Eleven

Luke listened as Aimee ran the eighteen-member Junior Choir through their two songs for the Baptist mural dedication. The school bus and the driver which they had rented from the Loch James School District for this trip to Roanoke sped along during the rehearsal.

"That sounds great, guys, but let's save our voices now for the performance," Luke advised them.

Aimee sat down next to Luke. "They do sound good, don't they? For only two weeks of rehearsals, they have learned to blend well and have memorized the music so they can watch me and keep together."

"I didn't get a chance to compliment you earlier, Aimee, but you really look lovely today in a French sort of way."

"Just what way would that be?" she asked with a grin.

"Something about the colors—the jade and chartreuse together in the print of your silk dress."

"Good for you, Luke. I did buy this dress in Paris three years ago. But thank-you for the compliment." She looked back down the bus at her chorus dressed in white shirts and white blouses for the occasion. With dark skirts and slacks, they looked very professional for the performance. "I'm trusting you to convince the church leaders that we need choir robes…probably blue or wine to distinguish them from the adult choir when they sing in church."

"I'm confident that the robes will be forthcoming, Aimee. Everyone is delighted already with your vocal training of our young people."

The bus driver was grateful for the barbecue following the mural dedication. If they only had to make a single rest stop, they would probably arrive home before dark. It made his extra trip easier, although he was well paid for such weekend work.

"I'm looking forward to seeing your mural of "The Good Samaritan', Aimee, but I'm also on the program. That's why I'm wearing my clergy collar. It seems that I am to pronounce the benediction."

"I did wonder when you volunteered as a trip chaperone. Perhaps you wanted to keep an eye on the twins was one explanation I gave myself," Aimee explained. "You do know what a superb boy soprano Andy has. Because that will change in a year or two, we need to make good use of it."

"I was aware that he likes to sing, but never thought about him using his voice for a solo."

"Listen closely when he sings the second verse of 'Softly and Tenderly'".

"I heard that in your rehearsal, but didn't dream it was Andy!"

"He wanted to surprise you, Luke."

"It does. His Aunt Lydia likes to hear him sing, but he seldom does when I'm around."

"Perhaps he thinks you'd prefer him to be better at sports like Mandy is. Was your wife artistic or musically talented?"

"Why, yes, Emily loved music, especially opera—but I don't remember her ever drawing or painting."

"So the musical ability comes with his genes," Aimee pointed out. "Clem says that Andy is catching on quickly to carving, too, which takes fine hand-eye coordination."

"I appreciate your taking such a personal interest in my son."

"I love Andy. In fact, I love both of your children, Luke."

This conversation was interrupted by the bus driver's pulling into a gas station for a ten-minute rest stop.

"Please be careful not to spill anything on those white shirts and blouses," Aimee warned the young people as they came off the bus. "Water won't stain," she added.

As they loaded on again, the bus driver announced that another twenty minutes would see them at their destination. A loud cheer followed his announcement. Accustomed to the beauty of the Blue Ridge Mountains, the students took the spectacular scenery for granted. The trees were beginning to turn yellow, the sumac to crimson, and the crags seemed as usual. That so many tourists came every fall from far away to view the fall foliage seemed strange to these native young people.

Of much more interest were the crowds of people and heavy traffic as the bus came into Roanoke. This was a big city to the Loch James youth. Luke stood and addressed the passengers: "We are here for a good time, but please remember your manners and that you represent the good people of Loch James. I want to be able to brag about your talent and behavior to the congregation tomorrow. We are invited to the barbecue afterwards, but will be heading for home promptly at five p.m. Any questions?"

Hearing none, Luke resumed his seat and helped the bus driver locate the Baptist Church.

—◦◦◦—

Everyone seemed to be talking and laughing together as they boarded the bus for the trip home. Quite a few white tops showed evidence of the barbecue consumed. The bus driver, Mr. Rudy, asked as he climbed into his seat, "Everybody having a good time?" A huge affirmation followed.

Okay, okay! Now everyone calm down. I need to concentrate on the approach roads until we hit the divided highway. Then you can sing again."

Aimee and Luke counted to be sure they had all their passengers, then gave the bus driver the high sign to pull out. Before very long, they were on the big highway headed for home. Luke sat next to Aimee again, grateful to have her to himself.

"I was very impressed with the talk you gave today about your mural and your conception of the Parable of the Good Samaritan. For someone who claims she doesn't go to church much, you have an excellent grasp of the New Testament."

"Well, you can blame Lizzie, Luke. She made Jesus' parables very vivid, and she really lives her faith in a joyous way that I admire. My parents used to make me go to church with them, but I hated getting dressed up and how the preacher used to drone on and on. Music was the best part of going to church."

"So what is your opinion of the church now?" Luke asked.

"Well, the pastor is certainly more handsome than the old one," she replied with a chuckle.

"Not only did I like your speech, Aimee, but I was quite captivated by how you energetically strode back and forth in your French dress."

"Oh, you and that French dress! How you like to tease me."

"TEASE is the word I was looking for," replied Luke with a significant glance at her which caused her to blush and change the subject.

"Didn't the young people sing well for their first performance?"

"Indeed they did, Aimee. And you were quite right about Andy's solo part. I'm glad he has found a distinction that is purely his own. But what about when his voice changes? There's no guarantee that he'll make an equally outstanding tenor."

"Let's take this as it comes," she cautioned him. "As you told us last Sunday from the pulpit, we should leave things in God's hands."

"So you were paying attention," said Luke, obviously very gratified. A silence fell as they watched the sun setting behind mountains.

Two months and I've fallen in love with Aimee, marveled Luke to himself. *Andy and Mandy have certainly taken to her. It makes me laugh to remember now how determined Mandy was to dislike Aimee and how now she imitates Aimee's expressions and actions! I'm not totally pleased with the number of Mon Dieu's I hear around the house. I wonder if Aimee considers me too old or too encumbered with ready-made family to be seriously considered as husband material.*

An hour later, the young people were quietly talking and some napping while the windshield wipers monotonously swiped the newly begun light drizzle from the bus's windshield.

"I believe I'll get off at the next exit and take the back road into town to cut off some miles," the bus driver explained. "There's not much traffic on the cold country road since they built the freeway." Luke approved the experienced driver's decision, and they soon were on two-way macadam through heavy woods. The rain had increased, so the driver slowed down somewhat. Suddenly a large, loaded logging truck came around a curve and its back end began to slide on the slippery surface toward the bus.

"Look out!" shouted someone. The bus driver veered toward the right edge of the road to avoid a direct collision and also felt his bus begin to slide. They slid downward into a small ravine for a short distance and then hit a tree head-on for an abrupt stop.

"Quiet!" shouted Luke into the ensuing pandemonium. "Now, if any of you are hurt, please ask the person next to you raise his or her hand so we can get you help." Aimee quickly recovered and went toward the back of the bus while Luke was checking on those in front closest to the impact.

"Mr. Rudy's hurt!" shouted a young man. "He's not moving and there's a lot of blood!"

Luke promptly went far forward and felt for a pulse on the bus driver. There was none. "I'm afraid Mr. Rudy is dead, son."

The young people nearby were shocked by this serious turn of events, so Luke said a prayer for the repose of the driver's soul. Then he took off his jacket and covered the head and the shoulders of the driver's body.

The logging truck had been pulled off the road a short way below and its driver appeared at window. "I've called 911 for help," he said. Everybody all right there?"

"No. Our bus driver died instantly when we hit the tree," Luke answered. He faced the back of the bus and shouted, "Aimee, can you and some of the boys open the emergency exit? The front door is jammed shut."

Andy's hand was up and Mandy was crying next to him. "What hurts, dear?" Aimee asked her.

"I hurt my wrist. I hope it's not broken. That's my tennis arm!" Aimee took a good look at the arm and pronounced that it might be sprained, but was not broken.

"I'll carry your songbooks Mandy," offered her twin. He also surrendered his belt to create a sling to support Mandy's arm. "Is that better?" he asked genuinely concerned.

"Gee, thanks," replied Mandy.

Luke came along to check on his children and was pleased they were caring for one another. He had already dealt with several bloody noses and large bumps on heads from the abrupt stop.

Dr. Stewart and Millie pulled up close to the accident scene in their car with Wendy aboard. Dr. Stewart was using his cell phone to summon wreckers and to inform the sheriff and waiting parents about the accident. Then the doctor climbed in the back door and hurried forward. He confirmed Luke's impression that Mr. Rudy had died of massive injuries when they'd hit the tree.

Luke looked over at Aimee. She was very pale and shaking with a delayed reaction to what had occurred. Quickly, he drew her into his arms to comfort her and then led her back to her seat. He felt such tenderness toward her as well as concern.

"Are you quite sure you are all right?" he asked. "You took quite a tumble into the aisle when we left the highway."

"I'm just shaky, Luke! I don't believe any of the young people were badly injured. I guess that the fact that it happened so quickly and many young people were relaxed and sleeping saved them from worse. Poor Mr. Rudy! I hope the parents start arriving soon."

As if in answer to Aimee's wish, a wailing siren announced the sheriff's arrival. Behind him was the Fire Dept. ambulance followed by a slower convoy of parents' vehicles. As the parents hurriedly parked and approached the bus, Luke called their youngsters' names like a roll call so they would disembark in correct order to be reunited with their parents. Finally, Aimee and the twins were dispatched with the Stewarts and Wendy. Doc had offered to check over all the kids for free at his Clinic to be sure all injuries were attended to. The paramedics were dealing with extracting the bus driver's body. Luke went with a sheriff's deputy to convey the bad news to Mrs. Rudy. Then he caught up with the twins and Aimee at the Clinic.

There were still three young people plus the twins waiting to be checked over by Doc when Luke arrived after picking up his car at the original rendezvous point. He went over and sat with Aimee and the twins. He leaned over to her and asked, "Are you all right now?"

"Oh yes, just a slight headache that can wait until all the young folks are taken care of," she answered.

"You do still look pale," he observed.

"I'm more concerned about my French dress," she worried as she displayed its dirty and crumpled skirt. "I just hope Lizzie can clean it up."

"It's funny that you didn't even notice your dress until you were certain the teenagers were all right," he commented.

"But I was responsible for their going on this field trip, Luke. If any of them had been seriously hurt, I'd never have forgiven myself! I feel so bad about Mr. Rudy!"

"Aimee, it was an accident. You are not to blame yourself. Actually, the youngsters had a good time, your mural is a grand success, and its dedication a pleasant memory. Aside from some bumps and bruises and an initial fright, all the young people will go home tonight more appreciative of one another. Mr. Rudy died instantly and did not suffer. He'll be well and truly mourned. And I certainly admired the way you handled yourself during the emergency."

Doc Stewart called out, "Mandy and Andy, it's your turn."

I have to go with them, Aimee, Luke said. "Please wait and we'll drive you home. I'll see that you get your truck later. Give me the keys, OK?"

Automatically, she handed them over and watched Luke's back as he strode across the waiting room and disappeared into Doc's examining area.

"Look at my sister's arm first, Doc," requested Andy. "She's hurting."

Gently and carefully, Doc checked on the mobility of Mandy's wrist and confirmed that it was badly bruised with a slight sprain and must be rested.

"You don't mind waiting on your sister all this next week, do you, Andy?" Doc asked with a wink at Luke.

"I can take care of myself!" protested Mandy.

"Why don't you two go back to the waiting room and send Aimee in?" suggested Luke. When they were out of earshot, he told Doc that Aimee had hit her head hard and still had a headache besides being very pale.

"Guess we'd better check for a concussion, in that case," Doc said.

Aimee appeared and Luke left her alone with the doctor. Shortly she reappeared with Dr. Stewart. "I'm glad to hear that you're driving her home, Luke because she should not be driving. I've given her some Tylenol and prescribe rest and TLC for a week. Call me if you get dizzy or something seems wrong with your eyesight, Aimee."

"I will. Thanks for everything, Doc," she replied.

Turning to Luke, Doc asked if he had any complaints.

"Not a one, Doc."

"Then I'll close up the office and head home myself," Dr. Stewart said.

Luke took Aimee's arm and hustled her and the twins toward the car. Lydia had heard the news about the bus accident and came to meet them as they pulled up.

"Can you put the twins to bed while I take Aimee home?" he asked Lydia. "And let them tell you about the accident. Mandy's tennis arm has been injured and will be sore for a while."

"Oh, you poor darling!" exclaimed Lydia.

"Andy has volunteered to help her carry things until the arms mends," he explained.

"All the young people have been affected by what happened. I was shaken up, but Aimee has a bad bump on her head. That's why Doc won't let her drive tonight."

"Don't you worry about a thing here," Lydia assured him. "Just get her home safely."

Luke and Aimee were silent during the drive up the mountain. Suddenly Luke felt her head lean on his shoulder. When he glanced down, her eyes were closed, her long dark lashes sweeping her cheeks. With her muddy, rumpled dress, she resembled a tired child after a hard day's play. A great tenderness swept over him; she had been so brave, but now she needed rest.

When he drove up in front of her home, Luke purposefully beeped the horn which brought Clem out of the house.

"Give me a hand here, Clem," Luke requested.

"Lizzie, come here!" she shouted to Clem. "Our little one needs you!"

"What on earth…." demanded Lizzie as she appeared behind Clem. "What's happened?"

"There was a bus accident and Mr. Rudy was killed."

"Oh, dear! I'll call Ann Rudy first thing tomorrow morning and see what she needs," Lizzie responded.

"Aimee hit her head but otherwise is all right. She just isn't permitted to drive tonight," Luke hurriedly assured them. "She fell asleep on the way home. Doc says to give her Tylenol if she has trouble sleeping and call him if she gets dizzy or starts seeing double."

By this time, Aimee had wakened and started climbing out of the car. Clem and Lizzie flanked her and began helping her mount the stairs. "Thanks for bringing her home," they said. Luke followed them in, saw Aimee settled on the couch under an afghan, and bent down to softly kiss her cheek.

"I'll call you in the morning," he whispered.

Chapter Twelve

During October, Aimee and Luke led the Youth Group on several consecutive Saturdays in gleaning the harvest remnant to distribute to the poor—apples, corn, squash, and sweet potatoes. They did this in memory of Mr. Rudy, the bus driver killed in the accident. After working so hard, Luke declared it time for a party to be shared with the entire parish.

Monty got wind of the plans and offered to supply the cost of hiring a band for a Halloween costume dance. The women promised to bake pies for a pie-eating contest. For the younger children, there would be dunking for apples—after the costume competition, of course. Aimee headed the decorating committee, and Pastor Luke was persuaded to read a ghost story to the young children.

Everyone was to come in costume, and merchants had donated nice prizes for the costume judging. Even the judges were to be in costume even though ineligible for prizes themselves. Great excitement and anticipation swept the Community Church's congregation.

What a dither about who was coming as what! Caroline Crapsey had rented her costume as Marie Antoinette from a New York theatrical costume house. It was complete from her high, powdered wig to her jewels and fan plus her high heeled buckled shoes. Aimee, in contrast, was coming as a gypsy girl with a red full skirt, white peasant blouse, yellow laced bodice, and black fringed shawl. She had castanets for her fingers and planned to leave her dark hair loose under a close-fitting multicolored turban.

Lydia had helped her household with their costumes. The twins were to be Hansel and Gretel with German peasant outfits while Luke was going in somber pilgrim attire entirely in black except for a starched white stock. Lydia herself was coming as Dorothy in the Wizard of Oz. She had dyed an old pair of heels red and made herself a blue pinafore. Monte would be a pirate with an eye patch and a gold ring in his ear under his tricorder hat with skull and crossbones on the front. He had even rented from a pet store a green parrot with a colorful vocabulary. (He hoped the bird might spice up the party a little.)

The evening finally arrived, the last Friday of October. The band played as people assembled and mingled, guessing identities and admiring costumes. At the costume-judging time, Aimee joined Monty, the church secretary, and the mayor on the judging stand. While the band played marching music, the contestants filed by the judges. A table of prizes awaited choice by the winners and runners-up. After the hundred-plus guests had marched around twice, a halt was called and suspense mounted while the judges conferred over who they collectively considered winners. Finally, after a trumpet fanfare, the winners were announced. As generally expected, Caroline Crapsey's elaborate costume was the prettiest, Mandy and Andy as Hansel and Gretel took the "most unusual" category, and three teenagers dressed as infants with pacifiers and bottles were "the funniest."

Next came games—bobbing for apples in tubs of water for the middle schoolers and a pie-eating contest for adults while Pastor Luke read a funny ghost story to the small fry. There was much merriment of all ages. A lot of pie slices disappeared in the time limit set, but as usual, the adolescent boys beat out the older men. Costumes sported wet fronts after bobbing for apples, but nobody seemed to mind.

Cider and doughnuts were available for everyone. Aimee was standing by the refreshment table enjoying a glass of cider when Ruth Johnson came along. "This is a good party, Aimee, and the decorations are spectacular. You're doing such a good job with our young people! I love your gypsy costume. Those have to be the largest gold loop earrings I've ever seen!"

Just then, Pastor Luke came up. Would you believe that some of the teenage boys don't believe I can dance in this pilgrim getup? Will you help me prove them wrong, Aimee? You do know how to jitterbug, don't you?"

"Certainly. My mother taught me because she said it was popular when she was a teenage girl. On rainy days we'd roll back the rugs in the parlor and dance for exercise. It was more fun than the aerobics they do these days."

Luke whispered a request to the bandleader and led Aimee out to the center of the dance floor. When the band began the introduction to a jitterbug number, most of the dancers left the floor to watch. The first time he and Aimee circled the floor, Luke was cautious about swinging Aimee out and bringing her close again. When he discovered how well she followed and how light she was on her feet, he really got into the spirit of the dance. As they dipped and swung about each other, the young people clapped and added catcalls. Aimee was flushed and laughing in enjoyment at Luke's expert leading and the sensation their dancing together was causing.

When Luke and Aimee finished and left the dance floor, Monty came over and congratulated them. "Luke, this type of vivacious entertainment adds to your popularity and in time, it will draw more young people to our congregation. Congratulations. Now, how about some slow music for Lydia and me?" Luke obliged by signaling the bandleader again.

Caroline Crapsey had watched as Luke and Aimee twirled in the old-fashioned jitterbug, much admired by the young people. When the music quit and so many applauded, Caroline glowered at the featured couple. Not long after that, she saw Aimee head for the ladies' restroom, so she followed her there.

"Hello, Caroline," greeted Aimee as they reapplied their lipstick at adjacent mirrors. "That's a gorgeous costume you're wearing!"

"It's more appropriate than that cheap gypsy outfit you're wearing!" snarled Caroline.

Aimee was flabbergasted. "I've admired gypsies ever since I was a youngster," she said defensively.

"Well, I believe in being a lady…someone who would make a proper pastor's wife," Caroline retorted.

"Who said anything about being a pastor's wife"? asked a puzzled Aimee.

"Don't act innocent with me!" Caroline snapped. "You've set your cap for Pastor Luke ever since you worked on our mural when he first came. You make up to his children, too. It's disgusting! A French artist like you would never make a good pastor's wife and that outlandish dance proves it. What an undignified exhibition!"

"But Luke asked me to dance with him to prove to the young people that he could fast-dance in his costume!"

"Well, your skirts were flying up and too much of your legs were exposed! It was unseemly for both our youth leader and our clergyman. My father was shocked and you two haven't heard the last of this."

"Oh, Caroline, I think this will blow over," Aimee said in an attempt to defuse the situation.

"Just you remember this, you little French gypsy. You are not a suitable mate for The Rev. Lucas Lee Carson III!"

Aimee turned and quickly left in tears. The attack was so venomous. She went into the coatroom, collected her car coat, and was nearly out the door when Luke saw her leaving. He quickly followed her and caught up with her beside her truck.

"Aimee, why are you leaving like this? What's happened?"

"I have to get away from this place! Carolyn accused me of being nice to your children only because I want to marry you! AND she said I'd never make a proper pastor's wife."

"Do you want to become a pastor's wife?" Luke asked curiously. He took her face between his hands to watch her expression as she answered.

"Well, Caroline sure does!" she evaded.

"I know about her ambitions. How about you, sweetheart?"

Aimee's heart beat frantically as she stared up at him with wide eyes. He could tell it was a new idea to her, so he gently kissed her on the lips and let her go.

"We'll talk about it some other time, Aimee. Goodnight and drive carefully."

Luke had just returned to the dance when he was called to the phone. It was Doc Stewart. "Luke, Wendy has just gone into labor and we're leaving for the hospital. Could you take Debbie home with you for the night?"

—⁓—

By midmorning the following day, Saturday, Wendy was still in labor. Aimee was in the maternity waiting area when Dylan Stewart rushed in, having just arrived home for the weekend from the University of Virginia.

"Has Wendy had her baby yet?" he asked Aimee.

"Hi, Dylan. No, but I understand that first babies often take their time being born. It's nice of you to be so concerned or did you want to see your parents? Actually, your mother is Wendy's birthing coach and your father is standing by to deliver the baby."

"No, Aimee. I'm here because I love Wendy."

"Well, of course, you do, Dylan. Your whole family has been so kind and loving to her."

"Aimee, you don't understand," he said urgently. "I want to marry Wendy and take care of her and the baby."

"Mon Dieu! Do your folks know about this?"

"No. I haven't even convinced Wendy yet, and we thought we had more time before the baby came to consider our future together. Wendy is afraid that my folks won't approve of her as a daughter-in-law, and they won't want to accept the baby as their grandchild. Do you think I could visit her now?

Aimee was not sure such a request was appropriate but suggested that he ask the nurse. He came back crestfallen. "She asked if I was a family member and when I said 'Not exactly,' she just looked at me and turned me away. This is so hard, Aimee! I wanted us to be married and go through this together."

"Dylan, often our best laid plans don't work out. Think of the plans your parents have for you and the impact of this new relationship on those family plans. Perhaps you should consult Pastor Luke about how best to tell your folks, maybe even ask him to go with you."

"Gosh, do you think he would come with me? I've been dreading their first reaction."

"I cannot speak for him, Dylan, but I know he's a good listener and will give you good advice."

Millie appeared at the doorway. "Aimee, Wendy is going to have to have a Caesarian Section because the infant is in a breech position. It'll be another couple of hours before you'll be allowed to see her. Do you want to wait or shall I call you after the baby's born?" Then she noticed Dylan's presence.

"Son, I didn't know you were here. Did you want to see me or your father for something? He's busy getting ready for the operation. What can I do for you?"

"Just take good care of Wendy, Mom."

"Well, of course, we will. How about you going over to Pastor Luke's and picking up Debbie? She spent the night there while we were here at the hospital."

"All right, Mom." He hated to leave but couldn't really do any good here. *If Pastor Luke is home, maybe I can talk with him. He's a nice guy and I think he might understand. I want Wendy to be my wife and to adopt her baby. Darn, I wish Wendy and I could have agreed sooner!*

Aimee walked out with Dylan, for she needed a breath of fresh air. "If your folks are upset about your plans, Dylan, Wendy, and the baby are welcome to come and live with us at Painter's Pond. I know Lizzie and Clem would love to have a youngster around again."

Dylan stopped in his tracks. "That's fantastic, Aimee! No matter how my folks take the news, it might be awkward for Wendy to go home to our house. I'll give you something toward her monthly room and board."

"Not necessary, Dylan. Wendy is a good worker and will be an asset to our cheese and herb businesses. She'll more than earn her keep."

"Thanks a bunch, Aimee! Now I'd better get moving to pick up my sister."

Aimee returned to the maternity waiting area pondering the import of what Dylan had told her. She sympathized with everyone involved and wondered how Luke would handle the delicate situation.

When Dylan rang the doorbell at Pastor Luke's home, Debbie threw open the door. "Has Wendy had her baby yet…a girl or a boy?"

"Not yet, so we don't know," Dylan answered both questions at once.

Lydia was right behind Debbie. "Come on in, Dylan. Tell us the news from the hospital. We're all eager to hear how Wendy is doing, for she's been in labor a long time."

Dylan came in and gave his jacket to Lydia. "Is Pastor Luke home?" he asked.

"Yes, he's in his study down the hall to the right. Just tap on the door. But first, tell me about Wendy," Lydia pleaded.

"She's having a bad time of it, and now they're going to operate," he told her. "They wouldn't even let me in to see her."

"Well, if she's having a Caesarean birth, we'll know before long about the baby," Lydia observed and went back to the kitchen with Debbie, where she had just started making lunch with the twins' help. "Please plan on having lunch with us before taking Debbie home."

Having been given an excuse to linger, Dylan went down the hall and tapped on Pastor Luke's study door.

"Come in," invited the pastor. "Hi Dylan," he greeted the college student.

"If you have a few minutes, Pastor, I'd like to talk with you about something personal."

"Certainly. Come in, close the door, and have a seat." Luke came around from behind his desk and took a chair facing the young man.

"This is about Wendy," Dylan began nervously.

Please don't let Dylan be the father of Wendy's child! Luke prayed silently. Aloud, he asked how things were going over at the Maternity Ward.

"They're operating on Wendy right now because the baby is "breech," whatever that means. It doesn't sound good and means the baby is in some kind of trouble."

Patiently Luke explained what a breech position meant and how it was dangerous for both mother and infant. "The fact that they're operating will end the trauma for both," he assured Dylan. "Is her being in difficulty giving birth the reason you wanted to speak with me?"

"I care so much for both Wendy and her baby. I'm in love with Wendy, Pastor, and have been trying to talk her into marrying me."

"Are you the father of Wendy's baby, Dylan?"

Dylan looked shocked. "NO!" he denied emphatically, much to Luke's relief.

"Then why do you want to take on such responsibility when you are still in college?"

"I love her, and I believe she loves me, but she's afraid my folks will disapprove even though they've been kind to her."

"So you haven't told them yet?" Luke queried.

"No, we thought we have several more weeks before the baby came," Dylan replied.

"Just how do you plan to support a family?"

"I'll quit school and get a job," Dylan offered.

"Most good jobs require at least a college degree," Luke pointed out. "Raising a child these days is quite expensive. I have reason to know."

"Well, for starters, Aimee said that Wendy and the baby can stay with her at Painter's Pond."

That startled Luke a little. "You've told Aimee, but not your folks?"

"Well, they wouldn't let me in to see Wendy because I'm not family, and I was really upset at that. Aimee and I were alone in the waiting area, so we got to talking. She mentioned that under the circumstances, going home with my folks might be stressful and offered to take Wendy and the baby home with her instead. She said Lizzie would be glad of the company and Wendy could help her later on with the cheese and herb businesses."

"Pastor, would you come home with me and Debbie? 'Help me tell my folks?'"

Luke thought for a moment. "Both of your parents will be exhausted after being up all night, so I think tomorrow would be a better time to approach them. Meanwhile, you need to be thinking and praying about God's will for your future. You and Wendy are both so young! No solution will be easy, but your parents certainly need to be apprised of your plans. Tomorrow is Sunday, so why don't we set up a conference at your home at about 4 p.m. if that's agreeable with them."

Just then Lydia knocked on the door to call them to lunch. The phone rang as they were sitting down and Lydia answered. "A little boy, Millie? He's five pounds, four ounces? Everyone's doing well! Thanks for calling, Millie. I'll pass the information along to Luke to announce in church tomorrow. Dylan's still here. He and Debbie are staying for lunch. Then I'll send them along home."

"A little boy! We have a little boy!" Dylan marveled aloud.

"Dylan, I think you should pick up some flowers for the new mother…maybe rosebuds and take them up tonight!" Luke suggested.

"Yeah, and see the baby, too!" Dylan agreed.

Wendy struggled to consciousness. She was still very tired, but content that all was well with her new baby boy. When she opened her eyes, she found Dylan standing by her bedside smiling, and holding a bunch of rosebuds, the first flowers anyone had ever given her.

"I just saw him in the nursery. He's beautiful…just like his mother."

"Oh, Dylan, I love you!"

"That's what I want to talk to you about, Wendy. Last week when I was home from college, you said that you were afraid my father and mother would not approve of our getting married. I've told Aimee and consulted Pastor Luke. Aimee said that you and the baby are welcome to come live with her at Painter's Pond, and Lizzie will help you with the baby. In turn, you can help her with cheese making and gathering herbs. Pastor Luke said that we are terribly young to be starting a family, so maybe we should delay getting married until I graduate. The big thing is that he's promised to come over tomorrow at four o'clock when I tell my folks."

"Gee, Dylan, I'd love to live with Aimee up on the mountain."

"Wendy, do you really love me?" Dylan asked in a serious tone.

"Oh yes!" replied Wendy. "I've loved you ever since I met you that first weekend I was with your folks. For a while I was afraid you were being nice to me just because you felt sorry for me. You didn't kiss me, although we enjoyed talking together. It took me three weekends to decide that you saw me as an attractive girl, not just a poor unwed mother."

"Then will you marry me?" he asked.

"Yes, if you mean both me and my son."

"You know I do, little mother."

"Kiss me, Dylan. I won't break." Dylan thrust the bouquet into her hands and kissed her long and tenderly.

"What are you going to name the boy?" he asked.

"How about 'Matthew' with 'Matt' for short?" Of course, he'll have my last name of Parker on his birth certificate."

"That's only until we're married, and I can adopt him legally," Dylan assured her.

"Oh, Dylan, I'm really happy! But I'm still worried about what your folks will say. They've been so good to me, but may not want me as a daughter-in-law."

Just then, Aimee appeared at the door. "That's a cute little fellow you have, Wendy."

"So you've seen little Matthew," Wendy commented.

"Yes, and he's adorable. 'Hard to believe we all start so small," Aimee added.

Pastor Luke arrived right behind Aimee. As soon as he'd congratulated Wendy and said a prayer of thanksgiving, Dylan took his arm, and they headed off to see Wendy's boy at the nursery window.

As soon as Aimee and Wendy were alone, Wendy shared her happiness with Aimee. "Dylan loves me, and we're going to get married! We probably will have to wait until at least he graduates next June, but I don't mind waiting. He says that you want young Matt and me to come and live with you while we're waiting. You're a lifesaver, Aimee! Thanks and we accept."

Aimee smiled and reiterated how much Lizzie and Clem would enjoy having a youngster around again plus Wendy's own younger arms and legs to assist them.

Wendy continued. "Pastor Luke has promised to be with Dylan when he tells his folks about us, not that Pastor is happy about the situation. It's nice of him to lend Dylan some support because it won't be easy telling them." She lay back and yawned.

Noticing that, Aimee said, "Good-night, Wendy. You've had a full day. I'll see you sometime tomorrow. As soon as you know when you are leaving the hospital, let me know so I can pick you up and bring you and Matt home with me."

Dylan returned alone. "Pastor had to go, but I wanted to come back and see you again before leaving. He kissed her. "Happy dreams, Wendy. I love you and little Matt."

"Good luck with your folks tomorrow. Somehow I know it's going to be all right. Thanks for the roses. I love you, too." Wendy was smiling as Dylan left quietly.

Luke was waiting in the hospital lobby as Aimee left the elevator. "Do you have time to have a cup of coffee with me before heading back up the mountain?" he asked. "I need to get home and relieve Lydia, but I would like a few words with you about Wendy and Dylan's situation since you are one of the few who already know about it."

"Sure. You go ahead, Luke, and I'll be right along."

Evidently, Lydia had expected Luke would need coffee when he came home, for she had two mugs waiting on the kitchen table plus a plate of home baked cookies when Aimee arrived. Luke took her coat and invited her to join him for an evening snack.

"Dylan told me about your generous offer to have Wendy and son come and live with you," he began.

"How old were you and your wife when you attended Harvard?" she surprised him by asking.

"I was twenty-two when we got married and Emily was twenty-one," he answered. "Why do you ask?"

"So you were about the same age as Dylan is," she pointed out.

"Yes, but I had already graduated from college," he replied defensively. "I had been accepted for graduate school and she was willing to work," Luke explained. "I take it that you are pointing out that in Dylan and Wendy's case, age is not the real problem, but that she is an unwed mother. 'Not that Dylan is the baby's father, you understand."

"Yes, I believe Dylan about that," she agreed.

"Well, Emily and I were good friends and sweethearts for more than two years before we got married. Her parents and mine were acquainted, and both sets of parents had agreed to subsidize us during our graduate period. She did have to work during my seminary days, but when she became pregnant with the twins, her obstetrician warned her that she was jeopardizing her pregnancy by working. Because she didn't want to ask our parents again for financial help, she didn't tell me and continued to work. Finally, she had to spend the last two months in bed and even with that, she developed toxemia and died during delivery. But Amanda and Andrew were both a good size and healthy infants. My mother's sister, Lydia, came for the funeral and has been with us ever since…a real Godsend! When I think back on those days, I remember how the other students would admire the twins when Lydia took them in their double stroller to the Harvard Yard. I couldn't help being proud, but I missed Emily so much!"

Aimee ached with sympathy for this good man who had lost his wife and yet been such a good father to their children.

But that did nothing for Wendy and Dylan's predicament. "You still think that Dylan should graduate before they get married?" she asked, bringing the conversation back to the present.

"Yes, I do. His last semester will be full of papers and exams, not to mention applications to medical school if his father's dreams are to be realized."

"Well, I don't envy you when the Stewarts first learn about the young couple," she said. "I guess I was lucky having parents I could talk to about anything. 'Guess that's why I offered Wendy and her son sanctuary with us. Well, I guess I'd better be going. Thanks for the cookies and coffee, Luke."

He retrieved her jacket and held it for her to slip into. "I'll see you in the morning, Pastor!" She quickly darted out to her truck and headed back up the mountain toward Painter's Pond. On the way home, Aimee's thoughts wandered.

How I would like to have and to hold my very own baby! I'd really like it to be Luke's baby, but he seems very content with the twins. Of course, I love those twins, too. 'Not that I would trade places with Wendy. I guess I'd better settle for what I have and be grateful. I'll pray for Wendy and for wisdom to help her until she and Dylan can marry and become self-sufficient.

Luke was grateful that the twins and Lydia had gone to Monty's estate to play croquet and have a barbecue that Luke would be attending after taking care of his pastoral call with the Stewarts. Rarely did he schedule such sessions on Sunday, but Doc's schedule was even busier than his own.

No further time should elapse before Dylan's folks learned about Wendy and his romance.

So concerned was Pastor Luke about the upcoming interview that he was not paying attention to the glorious fall colors on the mountains around, especially the gorgeous crimson leaves of the maples and the golden hues of the mountain ash as he drove along. He arrived five minutes ahead of the appointed time of four o'clock. The Stewart's home was a large and beautifully restored Victorian mansion with nearly five acres of gardens by the house. Beyond the gardens were fenced-in pastures for the horses kept in the stables. Luke parked on the circular drive and Dylan came out to meet him.

"I'm so glad you've come," he said nervously. "My folks are out on the side porch." He led the way through the high ceilinged entryway, back along a hallway, and then out onto a screen porch with casual, rattan furniture featuring colorful cushions, reading lamps, and magazines scattered on end and coffee tables.

"Hello, Pastor Luke," Millie greeted him. "To what do we owe the pleasure of your company on your busiest day?"

"I was invited by Dylan."

"I take it that this is not just a social call, Pastor," Doc said. Turning to his son, he asked, "What did you want to discuss with us that required the presence of a clergyman, Dylan?"

Millie looked apprehensive suddenly. "Let's all sit down then. Pastor, can I bring you something cold to drink?"

"No, thank-you, Millie. Let's let Dylan explain why he's asked me to come."

Dylan stood up and declared, "I am in love with Wendy and want to marry her."

Shocked, Doc asked, "Why on earth would you want to do that, son? You're not the father of her child! You have no responsibility for her!" He was close to shouting and obviously angry.

"Mark, please," Millie tried to calm her husband, "let's hear Dylan out."

The young man's voice was slightly unsteady, but he continued. "When you first brought Wendy home, I felt sorry for her. Since then, we've become friends and more."

"Surely you didn't take advantage of her while she was under our roof!" his father roared.

"No, Dad. I respect her too much. I love her, and she loves me. I want to marry her, adopt her son, and make us a family."

"And just how do you propose supporting a family when you haven't even finished your undergraduate degree?" asked his father.

"I could quit college and get a job, but Pastor Luke seems to feel that we should hold off getting married until after I graduate next spring."

"Well, thank God someone is trying to talk some sense into your head!" Doc said.

Dylan added, "There's something else, too. When I told Aimee in the maternity waiting area, she offered to share her home with Wendy and young Matt. She thought it might be better that Wendy live somewhere other than our home here while we are waiting to be married."

"So you have everything figured out, do you?" pressed his father. "What about med school and all our family's plans for you?"

"I did want to go to school, but now I'll have a wife and son to take care of."

"Oh, Dylan," sobbed Millie. "I believe that you are not the baby's real father, but what about all the church people and townsfolk? I've already spent time denying that you have anything but a platonic interest in Wendy. Now, what will all of them think!"

Pastor Luke spoke quietly. "I know this news is a shock to you, and I just found out about it yesterday afternoon. I believe these two young people love each other enough to delay marriage until after Dylan's graduation in June. Meanwhile, Wendy can take college courses via computer now that she has completed her GED. I spoke with Aimee last evening to verify her housing offer. She assures me that Wendy is a very intelligent girl who learns quickly. She'll be an asset to their cheese and herb businesses, even earning a small salary beyond her keep."

Millie and Doc were quiet while Dylan looked intently at his parents. Millie then rose and patted her son's arm. "We'll work this out somehow, Dylan, but we need time to get used to your news. Having Wendy go home with Aimee is definitely a good idea. Lizzie can help spoil her and the baby. Aimee's a darling girl, and I'm not home that much because of my job. I'll pack up Wendy's things so they're ready to be transferred to Painter's Pond. That's OK, isn't it, Doc?"

"I guess." He sighed heavily. "Dylan, you are NOT to quit school! We are expecting to help with your med school expenses and we will. But it won't be easy—no dorm living and you may have to find a part-time job."

Luke supported Doc's proposal. "My wife and I were both in graduate school when we were first married. We lived on a shoestring, but the Lord and love brought us through."

Millie chimed in. "It wasn't easy for us at first, was it, Doc? I worked while you went to school. Then I went back to do my graduate work later when Dylan was old enough to be in school all day. Remember?"

Doc stood up. "Enough for now. I think we can work this out. Thanks for coming, Pastor." Luke recognized a dismissal when it was presented, so he left to go on out to join his own family at Monty's lakeside home.

Dylan broke the ensuing silence. "I'd like to go over to the hospital and see Wendy and Matt now."

"Is that what she's named him?" questioned Doc. "Matthew was your grandfather's name."

"Wendy chose the name, but I think 'Matt' goes well with 'Stewart', don't you? I want to adopt him legally after we're married. Well, I'll see you later."

Together, Millie and Doc watched their suddenly mature son walk to his car. She turned to her husband and put her arms around his neck. "Remember when we told my folks we were getting married? Mother cried and Dad cussed, but we still got married. Not only did they get used to you, but they were very proud of their doctor son-in-law." They both grinned as they recalled those shared memories.

"Let's wait an hour and go see Wendy and our grandson-to be, Doc. I have some baby clothes for him to come home from the hospital in." The Millie added, "Although Wendy's baby arrived early, the church women are still planning a baby shower next week. After that, Wendy will have more than enough baby things."

"Well, so much for the plans of mice and men!" quoted Doc in a resigned voice.

Chapter Thirteen

Even the long table in the dining room at Painter's Pond would be crowded for this Thanksgiving feast. By now, the regular diners included Aimee, Lizzie, Clem, and Wendy. Four Stewarts—Doc, Millie, Dylan, and Debbie would be coming. Pastor Luke would be accompanied by Mandy, Andy, and Lydia. Monty's daughter was hosting a group of out-of-town guests at the Lake, but Monty would be coming later to have dessert with his new fiancé, Lydia. Lydia had been invited to both places, but she chose to remain with the twins for what might very well be her last holiday with them.

The star of this Thanksgiving gathering was young Matt in a tiny sailor suit which was part of the lovely baby shower given Wendy two weeks ago. She's also been given a year's supply of disposable diapers, innumerable hand crocheted and knitted items, toys, blankets, a high chair, and a playpen.

Lizzie said to Lydia, "I like this baby. Our little sailor is so good—he's even sleeping through the night already." She handed him to Lydia to hold while she bustled back to the kitchen. Everybody had contributed to this feast. Clem brought in the twenty-eight-pound monster turkey. (He made sure that Mandy counted the geese and was assured that none of them was being served up.) Lydia had brought a cranberry-orange relish which went well with Lizzie's special cornbread stuffing full of celery leaves and lots of their own sage. Millie's contribution was a sweet potato soufflé for the adults and whipped white potatoes for the children. Lydia's dessert offerings were pumpkin and apple pies to be served with whipped cream and vanilla ice cream.

Aimee's artistic touch was evident in the beautifully appointed table settings. The centerpiece featured real fruit and gourds surrounded by waxed small branches covered with fall-colored leaves. In deference to the children, grape juice was served for the initial toast following Pastor Luke's Thanksgiving grace. He prefaced the grace by asking Andy, Mandy, and Debbie to name something for which each was particularly thankful. Never at a loss for words, Mandy spoke first. "I'm grateful I'm getting a new uncle and Aunt Lydia say's I can be a flower girl."

Debbie, not to be outdone, said "I'm grateful I'm going to be an aunt to Baby Matthew."

But Andy said, "I'm thankful for Aimee and everything she's done for us kids."

Luke reflected that all three children had their priorities straight, that people are always more important than things. "Bless the Lord, O my soul, and forget not all His benefits!"

he quoted from Psalm 103. Then they joined hands and sang the Doxology together before sitting down.

Doc Stewart stood up, glanced around the table, bid everyone raise their glasses, and gave this toast: "To new, old, and extended families everywhere!"

"Hear, hear," echoed Pastor Luke, and everyone sipped for the toast.

"Now, let's have a round of applause for the cooks, and all the time it took them to prepare this magnificent feast," suggested Aimee. Everyone dutifully clapped.

"Can I make a toast for us eating now?" pleaded Andy. Everyone laughed, and Clem moved the turkey to the side table and began carving it so the meat could be passed on a platter. Bowls and platters circled the tables as plates were heaped high in short order. Lydia rose to replenish the hot turkey gravy in the big gravy boat.

Andy asked Mandy, "What is this red, jelly stuff?"

She replied, "It's cranberry relish, but don't take it if you don't like it."

They both passed up the bowl of sauerkraut, traditionally served with turkey in the South. On the other hand, the cornbread dressing found a prominent place on both plates.

Wendy excused herself to find a private corner in which to nurse Matt, who was beginning to indicate that he was also a hungry guest.

How beautiful and contented she looks! Dylan thought as he watched her leave the room. His father looked across the table and winked at Dylan as if he could read his thoughts. Since the young couple had agreed to wait until summer to marry, Doc and Dylan were once again on the best of terms.

When Wendy returned, Millie rose and took the baby so that Wendy could finish eating. Dessert would be served later when Monty arrived. While the women cleared the table, the men adjourned to the family room to watch professional football.

While they were shifting location, Pastor Luke asked Dylan quietly how his studies were going. "Better than ever," Dylan reported. "I have so much to work for now! I call Wendy every night. It's hard to be far from her and Matt. He's such a cutie and changes every week. I think he looks like Wendy. Did my folks tell you I've been accepted for Vanderbilt's Med School?"

"Good for you, Dylan," enthused Luke. "I've every confidence that you will persevere and do well. You come from good stock and now you have the incentive to buckle down, not only make your folks proud but Wendy as well."

The women had put the food away and carefully hand-washed the Limoges china by the time Monty appeared. Lydia dashed out to greet him and received a big kiss. They climbed the steps to the porch together and entered the hallway. The children came out to see what the new commotion was.

"Hi, Mr. Monty," said Mandy. "Are you the guy who gave Aunt Lydia that BIG ring?"

"Count on it, sweetheart," he answered. "And what's more. I'm going to give her a matching wedding band in a couple of weeks."

"Can I call you Uncle Monty now?" asked Andy.

Luke interrupted. "Slow down, children. This is not the time or place. Besides, it's time for dessert."

Lydia beamed at Monty and asked his preference between an apple or pumpkin pie.

"How about a sliver of both?" he asked. "By the way, where's this famous baby? I keep hearing about him, but haven't caught a glimpse yet."

"I'll show you," volunteered Andy. "Come into the dining room. He's in a padded basket on two chairs, but he's sleeping now. Shh! You have to tiptoe and whisper."

Monty grinned and followed Andy quietly. He gazed at the tiny boy and rather wished that somehow he could have a son, preferably by Lydia. He sighed and tiptoed again. Then he looked up Wendy in the kitchen and presented her with a U.S. Savings Bond for a thousand dollars to start a college fund for young Matthew.

When dessert had been served and consumed, Pastor Luke called for quiet and announced, "Lydia and Monty are being married privately the Saturday after next at 11 a.m. followed by dinner at Monty's home. All of you are invited as extended family." A chorus of congratulations followed.

"Next week, Monty and I are flying to New York to purchase my trousseau so I'll be a proper bride. We'll be honeymooning in Hawaii," Lydia explained excitedly.

"Don't forget to buy a bikini for the beach," Aimee suggested helpfully. Then she grinned as she saw Lydia blush.

"Well, Lydia and I have plans to coordinate with my daughter, so we'll be leaving now. Thanks for dessert and for feeding my bride. Remember, we'll be expecting every one of you at our wedding two weeks from Saturday," Monty said as he and Lydia exited and rolled away in Mercedes.

Doc and Millie excused themselves next, for Doc needed to make his evening rounds at the hospital. Debbie had arranged for Dylan to return to town later with Pastor Luke and the twins. In order to give Wendy and Dylan some private time, Aimee served Luke another cup of coffee in the kitchen while the twins and Debbie watched a television special.

"Now that Thanksgiving has been celebrated, Aimee, I think it's time to make definite plans for the Christmas Pageant," Luke said.

"But it's all set...like we always do it!" Aimee said. "You're not planning on making any changes before you've even seen it, are you? The Youth Group has already recruited the major characters for the Pageant, and the costumes are similar every year. Little Matt is going to be Baby Jesus, and Doc is going to be Joseph."

"So, who's going to be Mary?" Luke asked.

"Well...the Youth Group persuaded me to take a turn this year." Aimee could feel the color rising in her face and she hoped Luke would not laugh at the notion that she could adequately serve as The Blessed Virgin Mary.

"All I have to say about their choice is that they've chosen a very beautiful Madonna," he commented. "Now, since you feel we are right on schedule, could you please deliver me a copy of last year's program with the corrected names? That way, I can save the secretary from being overworked at Christmas time. She can run the programs well ahead of their being needed." He dropped the subject, and they both went to join the youngsters watching the Thanksgiving special.

"Thanks for the ride, Aunt Lydia." The twins waved good-bye as Lydia pulled away in her new car after transporting them from school to Painter's Pond. "Aimee will bring us home when we've finished rehearsing for the Christmas Pageant," Mandy reminded Lydia as she paused briefly in the driveway to admire the retired thoroughbreds in their pasture.

"I'll have supper waiting," their aunt responded as she started down the driveway and turned onto the road leading back to town.

A tall, dark-haired boy rose from a rocker on the porch as they approached the house. "Hi, kids," he hailed them.

"Hi, Ross," they answered. Ross Cunningham was assistant director of the Christmas Pageant and was extremely serious about his duty to run this rehearsal while Aimee continued to paint some Christmas orders with tight deadlines. Having Ross direct today met with Mandy's wholehearted approval. He was the object of her first real "crush" about which Andy teased her unmercifully. Pastor Luke had yet to notice that his little girl was entering the world when girls notice boys, especially older boys.

"Let's go along up to the cave behind the waterfall," Ross commanded. "You have his music and a flashlight?" he asked Mandy.

"Yes, I do," she quickly assured him with what she hoped was a winning smile.

"Then let's get started," Ross said and motioned Andy to lead the way. Since it had rained earlier today, the stones that formed the path were slippery. Much to her delight, Ross turned several times to assist Mandy on the way. Andy forged ahead, impatient to get his solo practice over with. He hesitated briefly at the end of the path on the large round stone before taking the usual leap onto the cave floor.

"Hey, wait for us and a light!" Ross ordered. 'Too late! Andy had already launched himself into the cave entrance, but in landing, he slipped and fell headlong onto the rocky ledge.

"Andy, are you all right?" shouted his twin. "Answer me!" Only silence ensued. "Andy, you are scaring me!" She turned on the flashlight which illuminated Andy's prone, still body. "Oh my gosh, Ross, he's fallen and isn't moving!"

Ross looked down in the light of the flashlight. "You're right, Mandy. He needs help. You go tell Aimee what's happened…and bring Clem here with you to help me carry Andy back to the house! I'll climb down and stay with him."

Mandy ran, slipping and sliding, back down the path. Ross took off his sweater and covered Andy's shoulders while they waited for help to arrive. At first, Andy just moaned and Ross told him to lie still, that he'd fallen and probably hit his head. Soon Andy opened his eyes. "Where am I?" he asked. "Why are my clothes wet?"

"You fell as you entered the cave here, Andy," Ross explained. "Mandy's gone to get Aimee and Clem to help you get back to the house."

As he was explaining to the disoriented boy, Aimee arrived breathless and carrying a blanket. "Mon Dieu! Look at the blood! Andy, I didn't mean for you to get hurt!" She carefully wiped the blood off his forehead with a scarf she'd been wearing. "That's quite a gash there. "I'll wrap this scarf tightly to stop the bleeding. Let's see if your arms and legs work. Does anything besides your head hurt?"

Andy sat up carefully. "I'm sort of dizzy."

"Just take it easy!" Mandy comforted him. "We'll get you out of here."

"Can you stand, Andy?" asked Ross. "Clem brought a rope to help us get back up onto the path if you're up to trying."

Andy, assisted by Aimee on one side and Ross on the other, gradually got to his feet. Mandy caught the end of Clem's rope and tied it around Andy's waist to assist him in climbing out of the cave.

"Lizzie's called Doc Stewart," Clem said, "and we're to get you to the Clinic as soon as possible. I reckon that means you get to ride in a bed on the back of the truck."

"I'll ride back there with you, Andy," Aimee assured him, "and Clem will drive."

"What about me?" asked Mandy, her voice trembling with sympathy for her twin.

"You can ride down to the Clinic with me," Ross offered.

She brightened up and immediately accepted. "Sure, I'll be glad to ride with you, Ross."

"Lizzie, will you please call Lydia and ask her to meet us at the Clinic?" Aimee instructed.

"Sure thing, Aimee. Here are a couple more pillows to make things softer for you, Andy. You'll see, Doc will have you good as new in no time!" Lizzie told Andy and waved them on their way. As she watched the truck and car leave, Lizzie thought to herself, *I'd better get in and call Lydia. She and Pastor Luke aren't going to be too happy about this. But kids are kids, and accidents happen. Andy's strong and healthy. I pray the Lord will help him heal quickly. May Andy's father understand and not blame us for the accident.*

Both Luke and Lydia were standing by the emergency entrance to the Clinic when Clem pulled in. While Clem hurried to summon medical personnel to unload Andy, Luke rushed to his son's side. "Andy!" he said as he eyed the temporary bandage on the boy's forehead. His color pasty white, Andy began to cry.

"Dad, I'm sorry. Please don't blame Aimee. I should have been more careful!"

At that moment, a stretcher and medical aides arrived to hustle Andy inside. "You folks can sit in the waiting area. Doc will let you know the extent of the boy's injuries after he's been examined," one of the nurses informed them.

Having followed the truck down the mountain, Ross and Mandy arrived after parking his car. "Will someone please tell me exactly what happened to Andy?" Luke demanded.

Ross spoke up. "Pastor Luke, I'm responsible. Andy was to practice his solo in the cave behind the waterfall. Mandy was to hold a light on the music just like she will for the Christmas Pageant, and Aimee put me in charge of the rehearsal. The stones on the way up to the cave were slippery and wet. Andy was so eager that he rushed ahead of us. When he leaped over onto the stone floor of the cave, he slipped and fell, hitting his head. Mandy and I didn't get an answer when we arrived and hailed him. Then in the light of Mandy's flashlight, we saw him lying flat and still. So I sent Mandy back for help. I slipped off my sweater and tried to keep him warm. Then Aimee came, whipping up the path with Clem behind her. She took off her scarf and wrapped it around Andy's head to stop the bleeding. By that time Andy came to, so we checked for other injuries but found nothing serious that we could see. Then we used the blanket and rope Clem had brought to help Andy back onto the path and down to the house. It truly was an accident, Sir, and we're very sorry."

Luke turned to Aimee. "Why weren't you with the young people up there, Aimee?"

"Well, Ross is my directing assistant for the Pageant, and I needed to paint this afternoon."

Luke stared at her, then turned and abruptly walked away. Mandy crossed to his side. "Dad, I sure hope Andy will be OK!"

"Doc will do his best, Mandy," he said trying to calm her. He was not actually very calm himself. *All that blood on his clothes! It must be a bad gash. Oh, Lord, please let Andy be all right,* he prayed silently.

When Dr. Stewart appeared at the door through which Andy had been taken, they crowded around him. "Andy will require some stitches, but it shouldn't damage his handsome likeness to his father," he said jovially. Sighs of relief were heard, while Lydia and Aimee hugged one another.

Luke thanked Doc and asked if it would help if he was with his son when the sewing was done. "No, I think he'll be braver if the nurses and I handle it. You just sit down and relax until it's time to take him home." Doc reentered the examining area.

Looking around at those in the waiting area, Luke said, "I think our family can handle things from here on. Thanks, Clem, for transporting Andy. Ross, thank-you for taking emergency care of my son."

Aimee noted that Luke had not spoken to her. She decided that a personal apology was probably in order.

Crossing the room, she said to his back, "Luke I'm so sorry about this accident."

He whirled around and confronted her. "If you had been with the young people as I have trusted you to be, this so-called accident would never have happened. Why, Andy could have been killed! What if he had rolled over and fallen on down the waterfall?"

Aimee was blasted by this accusation, and she felt tears starting. "I think you're overreacting, Luke!" she answered defensively.

But Luke continued, "Since your place is so dangerous for my children, they may not go up there unless I am with them. Is that clear?"

Ross and Mandy looked at each other in disbelief. "Dad!" protested Mandy. "Don't blame Aimee."

"We'll talk about this later when we have your brother home safely," Luke answered.

"You're justifiably upset right now, Luke," said Lydia. She turned to Aimee. "I'll call you later."

Aimee motioned to Clem, and they left quietly. She managed to make it outside to the parking lot before the tears came. Clem offered to drive and took her arm to help her climb up into the truck.

"Don't be upset, Missy. He'll get over it," Clem offered by the way of comfort. "The children love you, and the boy is going to be OK."

"Thanks, Clem. I don't know what I'd do without you and Lizzie!" Aimee wiped her eyes and blew her nose. "Let's go home. I still have painting to do tonight after I help Wendy put young Matt to bed. I sure love that little guy!"

Lizzie had a delicious hot supper waiting when they arrived at Painter's Pond. Unfortunately, Aimee had little appetite. Clem finished first and excused himself to attend to the livestock.

"Since Andy is going to be all right, why are you so sad, Aimee?" asked Lizzie.

"Because Luke blames me for Andy's accident. And I probably should have been with them up at the cave. As it turned out, I still don't have the painting done that I intended to do."

Wendy said, "Are you sure Pastor Luke blames you? He doesn't seem like the kind of guy who'd unfairly blame you for an accident."

"Oh, he blames me all right! His twins aren't allowed to come up here again unless he's with them."

"Well, his being a single parent and all makes him especially protective," Lizzie added. "Besides, he's in the middle of a very busy church season right ahead of Christmas…his first Christmas here. He'll think differently tomorrow."

"I hope you're right, Lizzie"

"Sure, she's right," seconded Wendy.

Aimee tried to lose herself in the unfinished paintings, finally going to bed late and exhausted.

Breakfast at the parsonage the next morning was special Saturday morning pancakes and sausage meal. Luke arrived late with circles under his eyes and had little to say.

Mandy, however, was her usual exuberant self. "Say, Dad, you're not still angry with Aimee, are you? Did you call her yet?"

"Why would I call her? Neither of you is to go up the mountain again without my being with you. That's final! I don't want either of you hurt up there!" He forked another bite of pancake into his mouth.

Lydia broke in, "Don't annoy your father at breakfast. He needs at least two cups of coffee before he's ready to tackle any problem."

The twins excused themselves to watch Saturday morning television. Lydia bustled about the kitchen while Luke enjoyed his second cup of coffee.

"Okay, Lydia, I've had my second cup of coffee and am now ready to tackle any problem. What's that sad face for? You might as well tell me. I know I'm going to hear about it eventually."

"Luke, when I called Aimee last evening to report that Andy was sleeping peacefully and might not even have a black eye from his fall, she was crying. Weren't you a bit hard on her?"

"Lydia, I don't understand you. Andy arrives at the Clinic all bloody and needing stitches after an accident in which he might have been killed, and you side with Aimee!"

"Even if she had been with the children, she might not have been able to prevent Andy's fall. Don't you remember when you fell out of the apple tree when you were eight years old and broke your arm? No one blames your mother, my sister. Accidents happen, Luke."

"Maybe so. Well, I'll see Aimee after church tomorrow morning." He stood up, put on his coat, and headed outbound for the church.

During a TV commercial, Mandy proposed, "Let's call Aimee and talk to her."

Wendy answered the phone. "Painter's Pond. Wendy speaking."

"Hi, Wendy. Is Aimee there? This is Mandy calling."

"She's out in the barn, but I'll call her. Hang on."

Soon Aimee came on the line. "Hi, how's Andy doing this morning?"

"He's pretty much back to normal, Lydia says. But my father was grumpy at breakfast this morning. He's gone over to the church."

"So, what can I do for you, Mandy?"

"We just wanted to tell you we miss you and we love you. Andy's OK, and we'll see you at church tomorrow."

"Thanks for calling, dear." As she put down the phone, Aimee wondered whether she would even go to church tomorrow. *It sounds like Luke's still mad at me. I wish I didn't care so much! Actually, I had a full life already before Luke and the twins came into it. Maybe I'll just stay home from church and get another picture finished.*

Right now, I'd like to just give up the church and the Youth Group! You try to do a good thing, delegate something to a young person to help him develop a sense of responsibility, and look what happens! So, where are you in all this, God? Please help me. Why did you let Andy fall and cause problems between Luke and me? She was crying again.

Wendy knocked on the studio door and entered with a tray containing coffee and a plate of cookies. "Lizzie thinks you might need a quick pick-me-up about now." She set down the tray and looked closely at Aimee. "Oh, Aimee, you've been crying. How I hate to see you unhappy. You've helped me and Matt and Dylan so much. Want to talk about it? Sometimes it helps to tell a friend."

"I don't think I can bear going to church tomorrow morning, Wendy. Luke is so disappointed in me. You know I never, ever would deliberately cause any harm to his children. I love Andy and Mandy. Even Ross called to say that the accident was no one's fault, and he was right there! I'm so miserable, Wendy."

Trying to cheer her, Wendy advised, "He'll get over it, Aimee. This is just a bump in the road!"

"You don't understand, Wendy. I love Luke! How can he trust me enough now to ask me to be his wife and mother to his children? Maybe Caroline was right about my not being suitable to be a pastor's wife." She began to sob again.

Wendy came to sit next to her and hugged her. "Give Pastor Luke three or four days, Aimee. He thinks a lot of you. I've watched him when he looks at you. He'll come around again."

"Thanks for the encouragement, Wendy. I think I'll turn in now. It's been a long day. But I'm NOT going to church tomorrow morning…not until evening for the Youth Group. You can ride down with Clem and Lizzie, all right?"

By Wednesday night, Luke was heartily sick of getting unasked advice from his adult parishioners and match-making efforts from his teenagers. Everybody in town, whether or not they attended the Community Church, seemed up-to-date on his love life.

"What am I going to do, Lydia?" he implored her advice.

"Why don't you call Aimee and ask her to meet with you about designing the cover for the Christmas Pageant bulletin and carol book? You could have her meet you professionally at the church and maybe mend some fences. After all, you did come down on her awfully hard about not being with Andy when he fell."

"You, too, Lydia?"

"Well, perhaps you should listen to some of this advice you're getting. Aimee is much loved in this community and you're the newcomer. Come on, Luke! Andy is doing well, and he's proudly showing off his scar. Shelve that puritan pride and apologize."

"Apologize? Any father would have been horrified if his son had been brought in covered with blood after assuming that he was safe and well supervised."

"All right, be stubborn. But I was so hoping that things would work out between you and Aimee because I'm leaving with Monty soon," Lydia reminded him. "Why don't you call her right now?"

Luke walked slowly to the phone. When it rang at Painter's Pond, Wendy answered. "Aimee," she called. "Pastor Luke is on the phone for you."

Aimee gasped, then wiped her hands quickly with a turpentine-soaked rag, and took the call. "This is Aimee," she replied.

"Good evening, Aimee. I'm wondering if you would have time to stop by my office tomorrow morning to give a final OK on the Christmas Pageant stage plans, and possibly from them design a cover for the Pageant bulletin." He kept his tone very professional.

Although her heart was pounding, Aimee replied in kind. "I believe I can do that. Would ten o'clock tomorrow morning be satisfactory?"

It was so good to hear her voice again even if she sounded a bit stilted. She was coming…oh, bless it! Luke didn't dare admit to himself, let alone Aimee, how much he was looking forward to their meeting. "That would be fine. Until then," and he hung up.

"Wendy, he called and wants to see me!" She grabbed Wendy and whirled her around in an impromptu dance.

"Did he apologize?' asked Wendy when they both dropped breathless into chairs.

"No, but it doesn't matter! He's missed me and wants to see me, at ten tomorrow morning!"

Lizzie appeared at the kitchen door. "What is this laughing I hear all about? It's been too long since I heard you laughing, Aimee. Let me guess who that was who just called."

"Oh, Mammy, I love that man so much!"

"I know you do, child. I have been praying hard about your happiness."

"He wants to see me. Gosh, what'll I wear? C'mon, Wendy, let's look over my closet and help me decide what to wear. 'Red and green because we'll be talking about the Christmas Pageant, maybe?"

Lizzie smiled as the two women moved off toward Aimee's bedroom.

—✺—

Pastor Luke was pacing around his office and watching out the window for Aimee's truck. When it appeared, he watched her alight and smiled at her bright red beret and matching scarf tossed over one shoulder. *She's even prettier than I remember*! He thought to himself. He turned and stood by his desk while his secretary, Miss Cora, showed her in with a knowing smile. Luke had been subjected to several lectures from her on Aimee's sterling attributes.

Aimee was carrying a sketch pad and bustled in, all business. Luke had the stage plans already spread out on top of his desk, and together they bent over the drawings. The location of microphones was agreed upon. Other than that, the stage plans were as customary.

"The Senior Choir sounded very good at their rehearsal this week," Luke said as he rolled up the stage plans. "I understand that you have been working with the Youth Choir, which is new this year."

"Yes, it will save the Senior Choir from having to climb the mountain, and they can lead the audience down below," Aimee agreed.

"I am most anxious to actually see this production for the first time. The preparations by people and animals seem well underway," he said.

"Clem will be grooming several lambs, and our neighbor will be bringing his donkey as usual," Aimee agreed. "The teenagers have their costumes as shepherds, wise men, and angels. They really look forward to this pageant every year." Then she opened her sketch pad and revealed a tableau of the manger scene framed by the Blue Ridge Mountains. It was done with brilliant colors and featured both natural starlight as well as artificial lighting.

"What a gorgeous cover for the bulletins and carol books, Aimee! 'Grand that you already have it done!" he complimented her.

"I told you that when I took on the Youth Group that I understood it obligated me to direct the Christmas Pageant," she responded. "Elder Lionel Crapsey told me to go ahead and purchase anything I need because our church wants to be proud of the Pageant. It's a draw for new people, and the collection at the gates will more than meet our expenses. The women of the church will be distributing presents and food baskets to the poor all over this county earlier that day and inviting everyone to come to the Pageant and our service on Christmas Day."

"I can't thank you enough for handling most of this," Luke said. You know how busy we've been with preparations for Lydia and Monty's marriage this Saturday. Even though it is a private family-only ceremony, I would very much like to come. It's at eleven o'clock."

"I know. Lydia asked me to sing with my dulcimer."

"Oh…that will be nice," said Luke, but he was obviously surprised. Evidently, Lydia was still secretly promoting his romance. How he detested all this attempted manipulation! *Maybe it will be hard when Lydia is gone, but we'll manage. I would like to choose my own helpmeet, thank-you very much,* he thought to himself as Aimee left his office.

Chapter Fourteen

"Dad, there's a postcard from Aunt Lydia in Hawaii with somebody surfing," said Mandy. "Boy, would I like to try surfing. Look at the size of those waves!"

Andy commented, "And the guy looks a lot like me!"

"Right!" said Mandy. "I'll bet you couldn't even stand up on one of those surf boards."

"Please, kids," begged their father who was missing Lydia's calming presence, to say nothing about her cooking skills. Despite the freezer left full of casseroles for two weeks, Luke was dreading the chore ahead of cooking for the three of them. At least, they were all invited to Millie's house for Christmas dinner, so he could concentrate on his sermon the day before Christmas.

The twins had already decorated the real Christmas tree he'd obtained on a tree cutting expedition with the men of the church. It brightened the sun porch and the number of gaily wrapped gifts under the tree increased daily. He was unprepared for all the gifts and homemade Christmas cookies, breads, and candy showered on his family. It would mean rationing the sweets over the holidays to preserve their teeth and general health—perhaps only after dinners.

Luke knew he'd be much more relaxed when the Christmas Pageant was over since it was an unknown in his previous experience. The traditional "hanging of the greens" had been done after church last Sunday, followed by a potluck. The closer it came to Christmas, the larger his congregation grew with people he had not realized were members. He'd stationed Elder Crapsey at his elbow after service to introduce him to the people he had not yet met.

On Wednesday before Christmas, his parents appeared for an unexpected visit. Although unexpected by him, it had been arranged as a surprise by Lydia, who feared he might become overwhelmed this week without her help. She'd even made up the bed in the guest room and laid out towels, all of which had escaped Luke's notice in the seasonal hustle and bustle. He was, of course, delighted to see his folks, and the twins were overjoyed to have their grandparents around Christmas. It did present a complication, for he had agreed to accompany the twins up to Painter's Pond for the final dress rehearsal for the pageant. He hated to run out on his folks who had just arrived, but Millie Stewart called to say she was delivering some gifts to Wendy and Matt, so she offered to ferry the twins to the rehearsal and back.

Over after-dinner coffee, Luke and his parents caught up with one another.

"Are you as happy here as you anticipated being, Luke?" asked his mother.

"Oh yes, Mother. The average Sunday attendance has grown twenty-five percent already. The people of my congregation are generous, forgiving, and quick to volunteer for any ministries I suggest. We now have a Junior Choir as well as the Senior Choir, plus a very active Youth Group. We've begun a daycare center mornings for the children of part-time cannery workers. Townspeople seem naturally friendly. The only fault I find is that they would all really like me to get married again and keep pushing female candidates at me."

"So, what's so wrong with that?" asked his father. "Maybe you need some help, son. I know you miss Lydia."

"Well, I won't get married just to have a cook and housekeeper. Now, let's drop the subject and enjoy the holidays."

Up on the mountain, Aimee was very gratified by how everything worked together in the late afternoon dress rehearsal. She was even able to slip away and be beside Andy in the cave as he sang "Silent Night" acapella with mountain echo. Since this was daylight, she hoped that the pageant would go as well tomorrow night under artificial light and with lanterns at strategic points up and down the mountainside. Would Andy get stage fright and not be able to project? When she voiced her concern, Andy reassured her. "Don't worry. I'll be singing for my grandparents, my father, and you." She gave him a big hug.

"I couldn't love you more if you were on my own!" she told him. "Now, remember, Ross will come up here with you tomorrow night. Both of you be very careful! Clem has anchored a rope to guide you across into the cave. We don't want any more falls. I'm still in trouble with your dad over the accident."

"We'll be careful, Aimee. I don't think Dad is still angry with you, but he has been awfully busy lately, especially since Aunt Lydia left. We don't see that much of him, but Grandma and Grandpa have just arrived to help out. You'll get to meet them."

"Good! I'll look forward to that, but we'd better get back to the house now. Millie is entertaining for Christmas and undoubtedly has lots of things left on her list of things to do. Dylan will be arriving tonight. He was a shepherd last year, but as a college senior, he considers himself too old this year. Since young Matt is to be the babe in the manger, Dylan will be somewhere close, helping behind the scenes and with Wendy, ready to rush in a bottle if necessary.

"C'mon, Dad! We have to get up there," Mandy urged. "I'm one of the shepherds to help Clem with the sheep and lambs.

"And I have to sing with the Junior Choir, Dad," reminded Andy. "We'll be alternating with the Adult Choir at the foot of the mountain near the main audience. Aren't those carol books that Aimee designed beautiful?"

His grandmother took notice of the name. "Is this Aimee the same one you were telling us about when you came to pick up the children last spring, Luke?"

Mandy broke in, "Yes, and she's the Madonna tonight in the pageant."

"You like her, Mandy?" inquired her grandmother.

"Oh yeah! She's really cool, Grandma."

"How do you feel about Aimee, Andy?"

"I really love her, Grandma, and she's taught me a lot about music and art!"

As his mother turned to Luke, he said quickly, "Now, don't start, Mother. We have to go. We'll meet you at the foot of the mountain when the pageant's over. Just follow the crowd."

Traffic was heavy even on the mountain road as the pageant cast and the Youth Choir, plus all the support staff assembled at Aimee's home. After parking there in the pasture, they moved toward the barns where the horses were stabled and areas designated for changing into costumes and warming up the choir and high school trumpeters who would accompany the angel's announcement. When everyone was ready, the participants moved out and filed down the mountain path to the stage area.

Luke chose a strategic spot from which he had a fine view of the stage. *This is a tremendous amount of work for a half-hour production!* He marveled as he watched Aimee line up all the cast and musicians before taking her place. Then she carefully received baby Matt wrapped in a plain white baby blanket. She was dressed in a flowing blue robe with a white shawl over her head and shoulders. Dr. Stewart stood next to them as Joseph, wearing a full beard and a red robe for the occasion. Suddenly the floodlights came on and the trumpeters blew a flourish. Then the angels swooped, their wings attached to their wrists, in an intricate modern dance, and announced the good news about the birth of Jesus.

Next came the shepherds with the sheep, Mandy among them, and assembled for a close look at the baby. Then the shepherds knelt, and the Adult Choir led the audience in "Angels We Have Heard on High" to which the Youth Choir responded with "While Shepherds Watched Their Flocks by Night."

Having moved the shepherds and their flock to one side of the stage, three kings appeared carrying gold, frankincense, and myrrh. They presented these gifts to the young mother and baby. Everyone sang "We Three Kings of Orient Are." The kings moved to the opposite side of the stage from the shepherds while "The First Noel" was sung.

Luke stood transfixed as the pageant unfolded. How many times he had read the Christmas story, but never had it come alive for him as it did this clear, cold winter night on the mountain. Saint Francis was right when he staged the very first Christmas reenactment with live people and animals in Assisi, Italy. It did indeed bring home the story of the Christ Child's birth.

And I can name each of these people in this, my new hometown—neighbors, and friends. It must affect the audience similarly. Look at how protective Doc looks as Joseph. Aimee is a beautiful Madonna. How tenderly she cuddles the baby as he sleeps peacefully.

Then Joseph raised his hands for silence, the spotlight fell on the Baby and Mother. In the quiet a single voice floated down the mountain. "Silent Night" sang Andy without accompaniment in a true soprano. "Silent Night" echoed from the cave. "Holy Night," continued Andy and was echoed by the mountain. A reverent hush came over everyone as the song went along in familiar words and tune. Gradually the lights on the stage were dimmed except for a single spot trained on the Madonna and child.

As Andy's voice floated softly in the air, tears flowed down his father's cheeks. *Aimee was right about Andy's voice. Come to think of it, Aimee is usually right. How I've missed being close to her since the accident. The twins really love her. And I truly love her! Why have I been so stubborn about telling her? Tonight…this very lovely night…I shall tell her and ask her to marry me.*

When Andy's solo was finished, the light came on full force. Both choirs, along with the audience, erupted into the grand finale, "O Come, All Ye Faithful." After a pause, prolonged applause could be heard from the crowd of spectators below. Pastor Luke hurried over to the stage area.

When Aimee saw Luke coming toward her, his eyes full of love and yearning, she passed young Matt to Wendy and came to meet Luke. He gathered her into his arms, careless of being seen doing so in public. "Aimee, the pageant was wonderful, and YOU are wonderful. I love you! Will you marry me?"

Dazed by this sudden declaration so close to her heart's desire, Aimee managed to push back the shawl covering her head and raise her radiant face toward his. She whispered into his ear, "Yes, Luke. I love you, too." Their lips met in a brief and gentle kiss that sealed their betrothal.

"Hey, Dad!" hailed Andy. "Did you like my solo?"

"Indeed I did, Son. Have you seen Mandy?"

"She's over there admiring Matt who is awake now."

"Mandy", Luke called to his daughter. "Please come here."

"Sure, Dad. What's up? I saw you kissing Aimee a minute ago. Did you two make up finally?"

"Better than that!" Luke began.

"You asked her to marry you?" Mandy guessed.

"Yes, Mandy, I've asked Aimee to become your 'wicked stepmother'," her father teased her.

"Oh, Dad! Aimee will be a good mother to us. I'm so glad!" and she hugged Aimee. Then Aimee turned to Andy, the shy twin, and hugged him as well.

"That was a beautiful solo, Andy. I'm so proud of you!"

"Well," said Pastor Luke, "it's time for the four of us to march down the mountain as a family to tell your grandparents and everyone. What splendid Christmas! Such blessings we have found in these Blue Ridge Mountains!"

Epilogue

Two Christmases later found Luke and Aimee's new baby son serving in the Pageant as the Holy Child. His real name was Lucas Carson IV but he was called "Lars" to distinguish him from his father. The twins loved living at Painter's Pond with all the animals and had enough activities of their own that they were not jealous of their baby brother. Lizzie and Clem had their own cottage slightly uphill from the main house, and the parsonage downtown was occupied by Luke's new assistant for the Youth Group and Outreach.

Lydia and Monty traveled often between his business interests in New York City and seasonal vacations in Loch James. She enjoyed hosting parties and business dinners for her distinguished husband. Their guests remarked that the Montgomery's still acted like newlyweds.

Dylan had married Wendy, adopted Matt, and was currently in his middle year at Vanderbilt Medical School.

Future plans called for him to specialize in Family Practice and return to join his proud father at the Loch James Clinic.

Aimee's art career had been enhanced by the murals she'd done, but she'd decided to only accept one commission for a mural per year. The remainder of her artistic efforts would be concentrated on painting the mountain vistas and folk.

www.ingramcontent.com/pod-product-compliance
Lightning Source LLC
Chambersburg PA
CBHW022207050726

47590CB00002B/674